A Candlelight Ecstasy Romance®

"I'M THROUGH, AMY. YOU DON'T WANT A FLESH-AND-BLOOD LOVER. YOU'D RATHER DREAM ABOUT A MAN WHO'S BEEN DEAD NEARLY FIFTY YEARS."

"You have your nerve," she screamed, as all the anger she had held within her suddenly rushed out in a torrent. "You took over my house as if it were your own. You seduced me, and now—after you've made a shambles of my life and my home— you have the nerve to blame me. Well let me tell you something. You're right. I do prefer my dreams about Harrison James. At least my dreams can't hurt me."

"Well, that's just fine. Keep on dreaming. Maybe someday you'll wake up and start living in the real world. Maybe you'll even realize that ghosts can't keep you warm at night. If that should ever happen, do me a favor. Don't give me a call."

CANDLELIGHT ECSTASY ROMANCES®

SO DEAR TO MY HEART

Dorothy Ann Bernard

Published by
Dell Publishing Co., Inc.
1 Dag Hammarskjold Plaza
New York, New York 10017

*To my daughter, Aurea and her friends,
Therese, Michael, Mark and Lester.*

*Also special thanks to Dr. Edward W.
Chapin, Department Head, Computer
Science, University of Maryland, Eastern
Shore, who graciously took the time to
imagine Harrison V's inventions.*

To Our Readers:

We have been delighted with your enthusiastic response to Candlelight Ecstasy Romances®, and we thank you for the interest you have shown in this exciting series.

In the upcoming months we will continue to present the distinctive sensuous love stories you have come to expect only from Ecstasy. We look forward to bringing you many more books from your favorite authors and also the very finest work from new authors of contemporary romantic fiction.

As always, we are striving to present the unique, absorbing love stories that you enjoy most—books that are more than ordinary romance. Your suggestions and comments are always welcome. Please write to us at the address below.

Sincerely,

The Editors
Candlelight Romances
1 Dag Hammarskjold Plaza
New York, New York 10017

CHAPTER ONE

"Miss Amy Kyles?"

"Yes?"

Harrison James V stood on the beautifully re-stored porch of an old Victorian mansion, looking into the cornflower blue eyes of Amy Kyles while silken strands of her corn silk yellow hair fluttered around her face in the breeze. For a moment he thought he had been transported back in time at least one hundred years.

"I'm Harrison James the fifth," he said as he cleared his throat and gave a nervous little cough. He was feeling more uncomfortable by the moment while the silence lengthened.

Amy was clearly transfixed. It was as if everything about her had come to a screeching halt, freezing her emotions and molding the expression on her face. She couldn't believe the resemblance as she scrutinized every detail of the six-foot-tall man who stood before her. Through the wide screen door she scanned his face, startled by how the mustache, shaggy brows, and rugged, craggy face seemed so familiar in spite of the short, curly hair, dark-framed glasses, and the easy, casual clothes. His skin was tan above the open-necked vee of his shirt, the sleeves rolled up and the bottom tucked in neatly yet carelessly, above a wide belt that held up his jeans. He wore running shoes, and she imagined his movements would be lithe and springy, but right now he looked perplexed.

"I—I've come about the Bible," he said, obviously hoping for some sort of response from her.

"Oh, oh, yes," she said rapidly, finally gaining control of herself. "I'm sorry. Please come in."

As she opened the door and motioned him to enter, her heart nearly stopped. This was Harrison James all right, but not the Harrison James she knew so well. She watched him enter her painstakingly restored parlor filled with green plants. Sunlight shining on the white walls from the huge bay windows lit up the room.

"Please sit down," she said a little hesitantly. "I was just a bit preoccupied with some of the research I'm doing for another part of the house."

"Oh?" he said, obviously interested as she flushed prettily in front of him.

Clad in a turn-of-the-century chemise made for today's easy living in cotton gauze, Amy was a picture of sweet, innocent reminiscence, its very definition. Harrison James V was instantly intrigued as he gazed at this woman who seemed to belong to a time long past and who seemed to fit perfectly into the house she had lovingly reclaimed and restored.

"You're doing a lot of work on the house then?"

When walking up to the entrance to the house, Harrison had thought it looked completely re-

8

stored, but now as he looked through a side window, he saw the weather-beaten boards on the back of the house and realized that the restoration of what had once been his ancestors' home was less than half-complete.

"I can't believe I've never heard about this place," he said, looking at her in wonderment.

"Yes, well, I suppose families can be split up and spread out in a country so big as ours, but when I found the Bible . . ."

"That's right," he said as if he had suddenly remembered why he was there.

Amy was fingering a large ornate timeworn book, an 1875 edition of the Bible, finely illustrated with engravings and embossed in gold. It weighed more than twenty pounds, and she was struggling to bring it to him. "Naturally I thought you'd want it," she said with a little gasp.

Harrison reacted instantly. "Here, let me help you," he said. His fingers fleetingly touched the soft flesh on her inner wrist as his arms went out to steady her, and they sat down together on a silk brocaded Victorian couch. Harrison found himself wanting to caress that skin with his lips but then stopped himself before his mind went on to even more erotic thoughts.

Opening the large book, she turned to him expectantly. "You see, it has all this precise family history," she said, "beginning with Harrison James the first, the man who built this house."

Harrison V moved nearer as she pointed out marriage dates and family lines of descent. He pressed closer as if he were truly as interested as

9

she, and he followed her hands with his own until their fingers, intentionally on his part, touched again. She flushed and shyly withdrew her hand, avoiding his eyes, while she continued to chatter about the significance of such records to him.

But as Harrison V watched the gentle rise and fall of her breasts, which were delicately outlined by her thin dress, and as his eyes followed the outline of her pouting lips and then traced the curve of color in her cheek, family history seemed of little importance. He cared about one thing and one thing only: the present and how he could get to know this appealing woman in the most intimate of ways.

"Anyway," said Amy, rambling on, "as I told you over the telephone, I really thought someone from your family should have it."

"Oh, so do I," he said, forcing himself to look away from her body. "I'm certainly glad I saw your ad in the paper."

"Yes, it's surprising," said Amy, who felt herself coloring slightly beneath his gaze. "After this wonderful house practically went to ruin when the James family sold it more than forty years ago, I've managed to turn up several of you—that is Harrison the first's descendants—by advertising the Bible for only his heirs."

"Well, I think you've been very generous," he said affably. "You obviously could sell it and make a tidy profit." He had earlier noticed the outside sign that said, ANTIQUES FOR SALE, BY APPOINTMENT ONLY. "And I'm overwhelmed," he went on, "with what you're doing to this house. Do you think maybe I might—"

"See the house." She finished for him. "Oh, but of course," she said excitedly.

Impulsively she took his hand, not really thinking about what she was doing and completely unaware of Harrison's electric physical reaction to her touch. "Let's start from the very beginning," she said, completely unaware of how beautiful she looked at that moment.

Harrison V followed her, mentally discarding her clothes as she walked. He felt more than just lascivious pleasure when he watched her hips sway, while Amy eagerly gave him a tour of his ancestors' home. Somehow, as she talked and explained, showing him her painstaking handiwork in the old rambling twenty-room house, Harrison kept enough control of his wits to ask a few pertinent questions. He soon learned that Amy was an instructor of history at the Eastern Shore Campus of the University of Maryland, which dominated the tiny town of Princess Anne, Maryland. She was in love with the Victorian period. She had bought this house in nearby Culbert's Cove and was refurbishing it with a large inheritance she had received from her grandmother. She was single and probably in her late twenties although she looked younger. She was obsessed with restoring the house with true authenticity and living in it in very much the same way as had the people who had built it and moved in more than a hundred years before.

She was completely captivating, Harrison V ad-

11

mitted to himself, realizing with a jolt that his intentions toward this creature from the past would have scandalized his Victorian forebears.

"You see," said Amy as she led him up the winding staircase, "the interesting thing is that this house had running water, electricity, flush toilets, all kinds of terribly modern things for the 1870s. I found the original plans. There are lots of things that weren't in general use until nearly fifty years later. But most of all, it has an absolutely wonderful charm, and I'm just fascinated with your ancestor Harrison James the first."

Amy was looking at a large portrait, ornately framed in the style of the Victorian period, from which a serious, much slicked-down hundred-year-old caricature of young Harrison V glared. He was in some sort of grandly decorated military uniform and held a pipe while he sternly perused the room where Amy slept.

"This was probably the master bedroom," she said, unaware of Harrison V's startled reaction as he moved closer to the portrait.

"My God, this is uncanny," he said, stepping nearer. "You know I've never understood this family mania of ours for naming all the firstborn sons Harrison James, which I, by the way, intend to put a stop to when the proper time comes, but he looks almost as if he had ordered it."

"Indeed," said Amy, looking at Harrison V genially. "I very much feel the presence of Harrison the first as the master of this house, almost as if I had to restore the beauty he created here so long ago. It's become very dear to my heart."

"Oh," said young Harrison, not really under-standing what she was talking about. "I can see you really are wrapped up in this." His eyes were lured by the huge four-poster bed that dominated the center of the room. The room itself was framed by a sunny bay window filled with plants. "I'm really glad to see that you like white and the light colors rather than those dark, gloomy shades that are usually used in a project such as this."

"No, that's the whole thing," she said. When their eyes met again, she felt a rapport that was strangely familiar. "When I went down to the bot-tom layers of the paint and wallpaper and stuff, these were the colors I found. This house was obvi-ously built to be filled with light and laughter and love. I can just feel it. I know everything was white and bright and happy. In spite of Harrison's dour expression over there, I'm sure this is the way he wants it, and I love it, too."

For the first time Harrison V began to have an uneasy feeling about all this. In the past hour he had discovered an enchantress who aroused him in every way, but he suddenly had the distinct feeling that she wasn't real at all. She was living one hundred years earlier. He couldn't stop his impulse to reach out and touch her, to be sure she was alive.

"What?" asked Amy, slightly flustered as his hand suddenly took her arm very gently.

Their eyes met, and for an instant it was as if currents of electricity poured through them. Sud-denly Amy squirmed, clearly confused as she sensed the eyes in the portrait of Harrison I on her

13

back. The snapping, happy, almost ebullient eyes of Harrison V, who stood mesmerized before her, seemed nearly identical, but of course, they could not be the same.

"It *is* uncanny," she said a bit hesitantly as she pulled away from his grasp. "What a striking family resemblance you have after all these generations."

"Yes," said young Harrison, following her glance at the portrait. "And you know, the funny thing is, none of my relatives has ever found much of a resemblance in me so far as my immediate family is concerned."

"Well, genes will win out in the end," said Amy with a little laugh that effectively lightened the moment and restored their earlier, more natural camaraderie. "You know I'm doing my dissertation on some of the things I'm discovering in this house."

"Ph.D.?" asked Harrison, impressed.

"Yes," she said with a sigh. "What with teaching and all this, though, I sometimes wonder when I'll ever finish."

"And what is the premise of your dissertation?" he asked, expecting something historical.

"It's all the gadgets and mechanical things in this house. Basically I'm identifying them and the time when they were used and then documenting the impact they had on society during that period. Actually it's an engineering thing tied in with history, and I find it terribly fascinating."

"You're kidding," shouted Harrison, more excited than he would have believed. "That's what I am. An engineer, mainly in advanced technology, computers and things like that. I've got a grant where I teach at MIT. We're into really fascinating futuristic stuff."

Disappointment suddenly shadowed Amy's face. "Oh," she said, "I'm sure that's interesting."

Seeing her face, Harrison immediately and instinctively sought a more romantic description of his work. "In a way I'm an inventor," he said, "a modern Thomas Edison." He laughed in an attempt to lighten the suddenly heavy atmosphere.

"Oh, there was only one Thomas Edison," said Amy as she gave him a pitying glance.

"Hey, what's with this attitude of yours?" asked Harrison, exasperated. "Do you think the world stopped turning in 1900?"

"I guess that for me it did," she said a bit dreamily. "Everything seemed perfect then."

"Oh, come on," Harrison said. Somehow his feelings about this young woman were very important and growing more so by the minute as his body continued to respond to her. He just had to make her understand. "You're a highly intelligent, talented woman. You can't possibly deny the future."

"No," she said, struck by the fervor in his voice. "But 1880 to the turn of the century was such an elegant time."

"Is that what these are all about?" He was fingering some slim paperback novels that were historical in nature.

She looked at him a bit strangely, and he again found himself mesmerized by her poetic appear-

15

ance. She was seemingly framed by the sunny windows and surrounded by a sweet motion as the breeze gently teased her hair. "No, those are Regency romance novels," she said with a little smile. "They're set in England more than a hundred years earlier, but that's also a very elegant period, which I love, too."

Help finally came to Harrison as bells of inspiration went off in his head. "So do these books adequately describe this elegance or whatever it is that you prefer?"

She looked at him blankly. "I'm not sure I understand."

"Never mind, never mind," he said quickly. "Would you let me borrow a few of these and anything you've got on the Victorian era, too?"

"I—I guess so," she stammered, clearly confused now by his behavior. "I thought you just came by for the Bible."

They left the bedroom and began to descend the stairs. "Oh, I'll get to that," Harrison said when they reached the parlor again. "But in the meantime, Miss Amy Kyles, I'd like to have the pleasure of showing you how the fantasy of the future can embrace the elegance of the past."

He felt his eyes being drawn back to the steps and up to Amy's bedroom, and he wasn't sure where these fancy words had come from. He just felt they were the right thing to say.

"I really find you a little outlandish," said Amy as she brought her hand to her breast, not realizing she was taking on a bit of a Regency pose.

"I'm not at all," insisted Harrison. "Let's just say

16

that being an engineer, I'm fascinated with everything you're doing here, and the fact that my ancestors were involved makes it even more compelling."

Amy looked at him for a very long moment. For the life of her she didn't know how the visit had evolved to this stage, and she wasn't sure what was going on. "Whatever," she said with a smile. "I'm around here most of the time. The Bible is yours to take if you want it."

"No, if you don't mind, I'd just as soon you kept it for me for a while," said Harrison. "I'm going to make arrangements to spend the summer here so I can examine some of your research—that is, if you don't mind."

"Well, I can't see where anything here could help with computer or space technology, but it is your family home, so of course, you're welcome."

"Thank you," said Harrison, preparing to leave. He was obviously a man with many things on his mind. "This has been a fascinating visit," he said when he faced her again.

Suddenly the scent of spring filled the room and soft May breezes blew warm promises at the two of them. Harrison could feel his fingers begin to tremble as they reached out and gently touched her brow. At the same time Amy felt as if something magic and sweet had come into the room.

"You're welcome," she said weakly as he turned to leave.

He hesitated for just a second when their eyes met in eloquent communication. A lecherous little smile played over his face, and he gave her a final nod. "See you soon," he said softly. He went out the door and walked jauntily toward his car.

Watching his progress, Amy glanced back up toward her bedroom, unconsciously comparing the man in the portrait that hung there with the one who was retreating down her red-brick sidewalk.

"Will you be here tomorrow?" he called as he turned and gave her a little wave.

"Sure, just give me a call," she said. She latched the screen door and wondered fleetingly what it was about this man that made her open her home to him with no questions asked. In the words of one of her favorite Regency heroines she was suddenly "most confused."

When Harrison reached his car, he was a happy man. Suddenly everything in the world was bright and beautiful. He was invigorated beyond words. A genuine brainstorm started to flood through his mind and then settled on something small and simple as he started his car and gave Amy a final wave.

Seeing her shadow behind the huge screen door heightened the general mood which had overtaken him from the moment he had entered her home. Wheels and sprockets and gears transformed by computer technology and grounded in futuristic theories began to take shape in his mind. At the same time strawberries, the color pink, and Amy's clear skin, blue eyes, and silky hair seemed to inspire him. He could hardly wait to get to pencil and paper as he drove to his hotel. It was only a matter of seconds after he had bounded through the door before he was completely engrossed with drawings and mathematical calculations that would soon produce the plans for a nineteenth-century ice-cream maker. Perfectly accurate in its outer antique charm, it in fact would do everything but eat the hundreds of delicious concoctions it could produce at the flick of a dial and the push of a button.

"Aha!" he shouted when the final touches came to mind a few hours later. He could do it. He could take everything she loved and turn it into something wonderful that could be equally intriguing to both of them. Then she'd be charmed with him and ever so receptive.

He sprawled out in a big comfortable chair, allowing his mind to settle into a leisurely daydream. He was filled with a delicious warmth as he continued to think about Amy. He could just see her on a hot summer day, making ice cream in the old freezer, while she laughed and flirted with him in a manner reminiscent of yesteryear. He licked his lips as he pictured her with her skirts hiked up and shoes flung away, one hand cranking and the other brushing away pretty drops of moisture that sprang out on her face and bosom above the revealing low-cut blouse she wore. The movement of her arms set her breasts into motion, and the whiteness of her teeth dazzled him as she smiled at him in obvious enjoyment. Moist, wispy strands of her hair blew in the breeze, and suddenly he was nearly overpowered by his desire to take her into his arms and revel in the warmth and moistness of her skin. Her neck was soft and promising

19

as he followed its angle down to her shoulders, and then he buried his face in the sumptuousness of her breasts. He saw her clothes falling away and could only imagine what a glorious sight the ivory skin around soft, rosy nipples would be. His hands traced her shoulders and then slid down the curve of her back to her waist. He yearned to hold and touch all of her as the very depth of his need manifested itself and carried him away beyond reason.

Meanwhile, Amy too was preoccupied with her thoughts. Again and again she looked at the portrait of Harrison I and then remembered the affable man who had just left her. From the time she had moved into this house she had felt content and comfortable in it, satisfied to dream about the handsome man whose portrait hung in her bedroom. Now with the advent of a real live Harrison James something had changed, and she felt vaguely uneasy. It had seemed like such a good idea to find the rightful owner of the Bible after she had found it in the attic. But now she wondered what she had gotten herself into.

Hoping to restore her usual peace and the happy ambiance of the house, she shoved an old-fashioned pot pie into the oven, the pastry was made from an ancient recipe that was part of her collection, and was filled with her homegrown vegetables. Then, moving through the house, she automatically flicked away particles of dust and then went out to collect herbs and fresh flowers from her garden. Young Harrison V seldom left her consciousness and only when he was replaced with the thoughts of Harrison I that routinely filled her mind when she went about her tasks. She was pleasantly perplexed by the situation. Nevertheless, she found herself smiling often while she continued to think about her afternoon visitor.

Comforted by the completion of her tasks, Amy felt both festive and nostalgic. Surely Harrison I would be pleased, too, she thought as she dropped her discarded clothes in an old hamper in her bedroom. She smiled at the frivolity of her thoughts. After a leisurely bath she dressed in a beautiful cameo blouse and a black taffeta skirt that fell to mid-calf. With her hair pinned up in an appropriate style she looked like the perfect Victorian hostess. Only the ruffle on her skirt and her modern sandals truly reflected the twentieth century.

Feeling as if she were the original mistress of this house, she indulged herself and set the table for two with exquisite china and crystal. She reveled in the sparkle of the old glass and silver beneath the glow of the chandelier. Fresh flowers completed the arrangement. She sighed in satisfaction and then went to the kitchen, where tantalizing smells indicated that the pot pie was nearly finished.

Across town, as Harrison V came out of his erotic reverie and reached for one of the novels Amy had lent him, he knew he couldn't wait to see her again. Looking at his watch, he realized he was hungry. The sun was dipping very low in the sky. He rubbed his head in exasperation and began to pull his rumpled clothes away from his body. Stepping into the shower, he gave a hefty sigh as he anticipated what he was about to do.

He dressed carefully but casually in a natty sport jacket and trim slacks. Then he went to the phone and dialed Amy's number. "Damn," he said when he heard a busy signal, and returned the receiver to the hook. After a moment's indecision he grabbed his keys and went out the door with a look of determination on his face.

Amy hung up the squat cylindrical receiver on the huge wooden turn-of-the-century telephone on the wall and smiled as she anticipated another sale to one of her best customers of her antiques, unaware that Harrison had been trying to reach her. She went back to the kitchen to put the final touches on the meal and imagined again that she wasn't eating alone. She looked out the windows and could almost visualize the firm tread of boots as they must have sounded a hundred years before when Harrison I came home. Feeling very festive, she paused as thoughts of young Harrison V intruded into her daydream in a most insistent way.

At the same time her eyes were once more drawn in the direction of her bedroom. Suddenly she had an almost breathless feeling of need mingled with a peculiar sense of guilt. Shaking her head, she firmly suppressed the feeling and distracted herself by straightening the roses she had arranged earlier in the afternoon. Feeling better, she bent over to savor the scent of the flowers and was startled by the sound of the old-fashioned bell on her front door. Trying to remember if she had made an appointment to show her antiques to yet another customer, she hurried to the entry hall.

The radiance of Harrison's smile seemed to fill the room as she opened the door wide. "Amy," he said easily, obviously enjoying her surprise, "I realized I may have acted a little outrageously this afternoon, and I thought maybe I should stop back and apologize. I hoped we might have dinner."

A bit overwhelmed, Amy searched for her voice.

A small bouquet of flowers filled his arms, and he offered them self-consciously. "I know I should have called," he said. "I tried, but your line was busy."

"Oh, no," she said, honestly touched by his appearance and manner. She pushed the screen door open and motioned him in. "I mean, no need to apologize," she stammered. "I thought our visit was fine."

"Well, at least we're of two minds," said Harrison, laughing slightly nervously while relief poured through his body. He looked about expansively. "I can see, though, that you've already filled the house with your own flowers. My Lord, I can't believe how beautiful this place is at night."

Amy accepted the flowers graciously although she couldn't help noticing the slight tremor of his hands as they brushed fleetingly over hers during the transaction. At the same time Harrison covered his nervousness and seemed to be instantly at home. He walked about as if seeing the house and its furnishings anew yet giving Amy the distinct impression that he somehow belonged there.

"And what do I smell?" he exclaimed. "You've been cooking."

Amy laughed when he twitched his nose appreciatively and followed the tantalizing aroma into the dining room.

"Oh, I'm intruding," he said, noticing two place settings. He was suddenly embarrassed.

Amy was more than a little nonplussed. The situation was nearly unbearable. She felt young Harrison's eyes traveling over her while she turned a bright pink. What would he think if he knew what she had really been thinking? "No . . . not at all," she stammered. "I mean—"

Harrison gave her an astute look and was suddenly elated as he noted her discomfiture. "Then maybe you were expecting me," he said, clearly pleased.

But Amy quickly recovered when she realized he had no way of knowing about her secret fantasies. "Now why on earth would you say a thing like that?" she asked pertly.

"The table is clearly set for two," he said with a wickedly teasing look.

"Well, let's just say I was expecting . . . someone." She managed a comical arch of her eyebrow that belied her inner turmoil.

Harrison gave her an extremely calculating look and was suddenly aware of her dress and demeanor as they were highlighted by the soft candlelight. "Not Harrison the first, I hope," he said, laughing.

Struck by his seeming perceptiveness, Amy wavered for a second but then looked at him brightly.

"Oh, one never knows in a house such as this." She sighed airily.

Now she was teasing him back, and young Harrison was more fascinated than before. Earlier she had seemed a poignant, vulnerable heroine filled with virtue and exciting sensuality. Now he saw signs of a tantalizing, sizzling wench, and he liked her very much. He again felt his blood rise in response.

"Well, you're obviously dressed to receive the master of the house," he said in mock imperiousness as he arched his brows. "So I suggest you get to it, Miss Amy. I'm about to starve." He accented his words with a little wave of his hand toward the kitchen.

Amy laughed, completely delighted now. "I'll see what I can do," she said as she looked for something in which to arrange the bouquet he had brought.

Harrison watched as she reached high for a vase and was again struck by her beauty, which was only heightened by the lace and sheer trim of her high-collared Victorian blouse. "Seriously," he said as he went to give her some assistance, "I don't mean to intrude. I wanted to take you out."

"No," said Amy, finally relaxing. "You're not intruding at all. The table set for two is good for my antiques business. It gives the house an authentic touch." She wondered why she hadn't thought of that excuse sooner as she realized how silly she had felt in these past few moments.

"You're sure," he said as he gave her another appraising look.

"Very sure," she answered, and looked at him gaily. "But now that you're here, I'd love to have you stay and give me a good reason to put the dining room to use."

"Great," he said with enthusiasm.

He had very much liked the idea that she was expecting him. But obviously it made sense to dress and play a part that would enhance one's livelihood, and his admiration was very much intact as he too relaxed. "I was hoping to learn a lot more about you and this house. I have to admit this is my first experience at being an honest-to-God descendant. It sort of creeps up on you and makes you want to learn more and more."

"I know," she said with a happy smile. "My whole life, as you can see, is devoted to history."

The rest of the evening was like a dream. Harrison was fascinated with the engineering antiquities of the house, and Amy was jokingly tolerant of his wild ideas for modern adaptations while she respectfully pointed out that they probably had already been transformed in one way or another.

"I know what you're saying," said Harrison as they finished the delicious meal. He had to admit that there was a certain charm and elegance that were created by the old-fashioned china and silver and the soft light of the crystal chandelier. "But as you say, so many modern things have lost their initial charm. That's why something so simple as that old coffee mill in the kitchen or an ice-cream freezer can be modernized and still—"

"But why," asked Amy, cutting him off, "make it so complicated? What's wrong with getting a little exercise and then simply enjoying plain vanilla ice cream?"

"You don't know what fun you're missing," he said.

"And I'm not sure I want to know," she said in mock seriousness while they rose.

Waving him away when he made motions to help clear the table, she reached for an ornate decanter and matching glasses. "After-dinner liqueur?" she asked.

"Why not?" he said as he went to join her. At the same time he was visualizing a marvelous way in which the table could be cleared and all the kitchen tasks taken care of while they enjoyed their drinks, a way that wouldn't compromise the house. Smiling, he knew he was going to have a wonderful time at his drafting board over the next few months.

They settled into the comfort of the library, and Amy felt a great sense of satisfaction. Their discussion returned to the family Bible and Harrison's ties to the house, evolving into Amy's plans for her summer restoration projects and her dissertation.

"It sounds like you could use some help," he said as he looked at her appreciatively. "You know I'm really pleased that you're willing to let me study with you. I can't believe how much I'm looking forward to it." His eyes were soft with anticipation.

"Just so long as we understand each other," she said, feeling herself growing a little warm. "This is no place for slick, modern contraptions."

"Oh, of course not." He laughed. "After all, this

is the home of the first Harrison James, my illustrious ancestor. How could I ever forget that!"

She smiled and shook her head. "You know what I mean," she said.

But she had to admit that she was delighted by his sense of humor, and as she looked at him in appreciation, she again had an almost overwhelming feeling of déjà vu. There was no doubt about it. The character of the house was greatly enhanced by the presence of a man who really appreciated it. In a moment of sheer fantasy, when she looked at Harrison and was captivated anew by his charm, she truly could almost believe Harrison I had actually returned home.

As the evening drew to a close, they both were basking in the warmth of the liqueur and the easy rapport they had established. There was an aura of contentment that seemed to surround them as she reluctantly walked with him to the door.

"I've had such a good time," he said, turning toward her. "I'm glad you invited me to stay for dinner."

He stepped closer and reached for her hand. Then he pulled her nearer, reveling in the perfume of her skin and the silkiness of her hair. Their lips were only inches apart as she met his eyes. His mouth captured hers, and in an instant a wild crescendo of passion pulled them into a molten embrace.

"Oh, yes!" gasped Harrison as he felt everything warm and vulnerable in her come toward him in a melting, lingering way.

His lips left tracks of fire over her features and

Amy responded with a practiced ardor the way she had so many times before in her most secret dreams until suddenly she realized this was no dream. It was really happening.

"Oh, forgive me," she said, pulling away. "I forgot for a moment—"

"No," said Harrison. He looked at her compellingly. "There's nothing to forgive."

He swept her into his arms again, and Amy was whisked far above every pinnacle of ecstasy she had ever known. It was an encounter almost beyond her simple comprehension. There was magic in his lips, and Amy responded with emotion that she had only fantasized about until that moment. Harrison was as physically overwhelmed as she was. He showered her face with warm, tender kisses and then gave in to the intensity of his desire. His tongue plunged through her lips and then parried with hers in fiery delight. His hands trailed down her shoulders as his lips then brushed her ear.

"I don't think I want to go home," he murmured as his touch sent shivers of delight through her.

"Maybe you are home." She sighed, not even realizing what she had said.

"Do you mean that?" he asked. His hands slid down over her waist and then moved up to the soft curve of her breast. He felt her nipples harden beneath his fingers, and he looked expectantly toward the stairs.

She opened her lips to receive his ardor and then suddenly stopped, coming to her senses. "No, no, this is all very confusing," she said. Suddenly,

29

for some reason, she felt very guilty. "I really don't know what's gotten into me," she went on breathlessly.

Intuitively reading the situation with more sensitivity than he knew he had, Harrison held her away from him. Although his hunger for her was nearly overpowering, he saw her perplexity and sought to ease it. "I'll see you tomorrow," he said softly. "And don't worry. We have plenty of time to figure this out." He pulled her close for one sweet and gentle kiss and then left, not trusting himself to speak again.

Amy dazedly watched him leave before she closed the door and locked it. She began to climb the steps. When she reached her room and lay down in the middle of the bed, Harrison James I glared out at her. "Have you come back?" she whispered. "Have you really?"

Then she sat up with a jerk, feeling ridiculous. There was no way a hip, modern MIT computer professor or inventor or whatever he was who happened to look like Harrison I could ever truly be anything like him. At least she didn't think he could. But when she touched her lips and remembered his caresses, she couldn't help wondering if she might be wrong.

CHAPTER TWO

Forcing herself to return to reality, Amy rose from the bed. Wistfully she traced the ornate carving on the tall bedposts and then looked away from the portrait on the wall. Taking a big breath, she went into the bathroom and splashed her face with water, hoping to wash away the vestiges of her momentary lapse of reason. Seeing herself above the high collar of the lacy blouse, she reddened and hastily began to remove it. She changed rapidly into a silk dressing gown and went back downstairs.

As she extinguished candles and tidied up, she had a warm feeling, recalling her visitor. Going through the parlor with a final flick of her feather duster, she reveled in the fragrance of wood and fine furniture polish. There was a marvelous mixture of old and new scents as a result of the ongoing renovation of the house and her careful care of the antiques that were part of every completed room.

She felt a deep satisfaction a little while later, knowing the kitchen was all straight and ready for breakfast. The china and silver had been carefully washed and put away. Everything was in readiness again should the master return unexpectedly.

Silly woman, she admonished herself, smiling slightly.

But what was the harm? she thought as she headed back to the library, which was always warm and cheerfully comfortable. It was one of her favorite rooms. She sat down in one of the huge wing chairs that flanked the fireplace. She ran her hands over the rich tapestried upholstery and thought about the lively conversation she had enjoyed a little earlier with young Harrison. Then she reached out to examine her most cherished possession, a small portrait of Harrison I done in pastel oils. Like the other painting, it had a wide, ornate wooden frame, but the portrait was done in a softer diffused light, and the subject seemed younger and more sensitive, almost approachable, in this pose.

As she gazed at the picture and thought of the many times she had sat here, Amy looked out through the screened French doors that opened onto the side garden and imagined that the roses growing there must have been enjoyed by others who had lived here many years before. The contrast of the flowers with the lush green of the leaves always transported her in some special way. But now, as she once more perused the portrait, she saw an even more real smile, enlivened by dancing eyes and for just a second a glimpse of dark-framed glasses.

Oh, yes, let's get silly. She chastised herself one more time. She continued to take in all the scents of the late summer night blending with the fragrance of the house. She reached for a knitting project that filled a round, squat basket near her chair. After spreading it out and quickly checking to see where she'd left off, she grasped the needles and strung the yarn through her fingers, automatically adjusting it to the right tension.

This was a fun project patterned after a comfortable African Kutu, a caftanlike garment. Amy could just imagine how Harrison I, a brave sea captain, might have brought back such a garment from his far journeys as she examined the pointed capelet that flowed out over the arms in place of sleeves. While she rhythmically worked the soft mohair yarn in her version of an elegant winter dress, she could almost hear steps again as they might have sounded bounding up the red-brick walk.

It was her favorite fantasy, although sometimes it embarrassed her terribly. She would imagine Harrison I returning home from an extended ocean voyage. She would meet him at the door, breathless with joy and anticipation, and fall into his arms. He would shower her with gifts from exotic lands and kiss her tenderly. Finally, they would mount the stairs together, hand in hand, and when they reached the bedroom, he would love her so delicately and tenderly and completely that Amy would cry from sheer happiness.

Feeling a little silly, she finished her row of knitting and then got up with a sigh. *What would we do without fantasy?* she thought wryly. She paused and once more gazed around the room, taking one last look at the small portrait. Wistfully she turned away. "That must have been such a wonderful time," she said aloud.

She headed back up the stairs slowly, refusing to allow herself to dwell on her fantasies. *I must remember to suggest this period for some of my students' research papers next year,* she thought, firmly turning her mind in a more realistic direction. *I mean, the period, not the activity,* she added as she felt the beginning of a flush, and then smiled at the naughtiness of the whole concept.

Moments later she lay in the middle of her wonderfully soft old feather mattress. It was narrow compared to modern versions, but she loved it. Her hand trailed across the vanilla-colored sheet, which was trimmed in heavy lace. Sighing, she looked up at the portrait, which was slightly luminescent in the full moonlight, and gave in to yet another dream, one that always afforded her a sweet comfort. While drowsiness overtook her, she could almost feel the roughness of his sunburned hand as his fingers curled around hers. She could almost feel the warmth of his body and hear his quiet breathing, which always made her feel safe, and loved.

Yes, she thought as she once more imagined the sweetness of Harrison I's lips. Who could possibly want anything more from life when she could have this feeling and all the happiness that went with it whenever she liked? *You can be sure, Harrison, that this house will always be just the way you created it.* She sighed.

After that she was carried away in wild dreams

filled with passion and emotion as her unconscious mind reached out to a man long dead. At times, though, the face in her dreams became a little more animated and the eyes that she so adored in the small portrait in the library were occasionally framed by dark-rimmed glasses.

The next morning as always she arose refreshed and happy. Going about her tasks in the house, she prepared a hearty breakfast in anticipation of some fairly strenuous work, including stripping the walls in one of the unfinished upstairs rooms. Impressed with the stacked lumber construction method that had allowed the house to stand solidly against decades of gales and hurricanes, she was hoping to replace where necessary the original gypsum plaster which covered cypress laths. Annoyed anew that the house had been allowed to deteriorate, she dressed in old jeans and shirt and covered her hair with a bandanna.

After she had finished her coffee, she took another quick look at the house, and satisfied that everything in the refurbished rooms was in order, she glanced at the Bible. *I wonder why he didn't take it with him,* she thought. She went into the parlor. For some reason she felt compelled to sit down and examine the Bible again, even though it was something she had done many times before. When she opened the pages, young Harrison V came into full focus in her mind. She smiled as she remembered his energy and enthusiasm. *Oh, well,* she thought, envisioning his return. *He's certainly a nice diversion, and giving him the Bible is the right thing to do.*

As she looked at the flyleaf, she saw names of people whom she had never known, yet who somehow seemed familiar. She remembered that was the way she had felt almost from the moment of her discovery of the Bible. She would never forget it. On a cold, drizzly day, just shortly after she had completed the downstairs refurbishing about five or six months before, she had headed upstairs to the third floor, trying to decide on her next remodeling direction, when her steps led her up to the attic. Somehow she had always avoided exploring it fully, but that day she had felt the time had come. It turned out to be a virtual treasure trove. Not only had she found the small picture of Harrison I, which she immediately cherished, but nestled next to it, in an old trunk shoved deep into the rafters, was the Bible. From the moment she touched it, Amy had known she must try to reach the people who had ties to this house. It was an overwhelming, compelling sensation, much like the feeling that had accompanied her discovery of the large portrait when she first moved into the house. After she had dusted off both the small portrait and the Bible, taking her time to examine them carefully, she had found many other relics. Among them were the very practical cast-iron pots that she had painstakingly cleaned and cured and now used for much of her cooking.

She smiled as she realized how good it made her feel to use these things and how satisfying it was to identify some of the other old gadgets she had found and then to try to make them work again. The passing on of the Bible to the rightful heirs also seemed to be necessary to her. It never occurred to her to keep it for herself.

Remembering then the project she had planned for the day, she closed the Bible with a sigh, flicked away a grain of dust from its cover, and headed up the stairs to the grim, sad part of the house that desperately needed attention. It wasn't long before stripping away water-stained portions of the old wall, she was coughing and covered with dust. She ripped and tugged to the constant accompaniment of clatter and crash. She grunted in exasperation as the quality of the old workmanship sometimes proved to be a nemesis. It wasn't any surprise that she didn't hear the doorbell or the particularly loud and persistent knocking on the side doors.

The room was filled with dust and resembled a war zone in the midst of intense bombing when the ceiling gave in and came crumbling down all around Amy, causing her to fall to the floor in a coughing fit. She never heard the steps racing up the stairway and down the narrow hall.

"What in God's name are you up to?" shouted Harrison V as he lurched through the door.

"What?" said Amy, startled.

She cleared a little of the dust from her face and squinted up through the mess.

"What are you doing?" he asked again.

The sweet, old-time ingenue he had met yesterday had turned into a filthy woman grubbing in the dirt as she wiped her eyes with dust-covered hands and looked up at him in confusion.

"What does it look like I'm doing and how did

you get in here?" she asked at the same time. Accepting his hand, she allowed him to pull her to her feet while she continued to dust some of the grime off.

Touching her immediately made Harrison recall the lascivious thoughts that he was determined to make realities as soon as possible. But looking at her smudged attire, he couldn't help smiling. "I was coming to see you again when it sounded like the whole place was coming down. I called and rattled the doors, and then, when I saw white stuff coming out of the window, I got in through the kitchen and—"

She looked at him and began to laugh.

"My God, you scared me to death!" he said.

"How touching," she replied as she dropped her lashes.

Harrison immediately visualized carrying her to the old bathtub down the hall and washing all the dirt off her body. He'd do it slowly and leisurely until her pink skin glowed again. Licking his lips, he barely managed to refocus his thoughts while he looked around distastefully. "Why are you doing this by yourself? This is dangerous."

"Because I want to and I know what I'm doing," she said as she met his eyes directly.

"Of course you do," he said, eyeing the rubble that filled the room and crunched beneath their feet. He waved the dust away, thankful that it was finally beginning to clear. "There are people who could help you with this."

"I *want* to do it myself," she said firmly.

"But that could take forever," he answered in

disbelief. It suddenly began to dawn on him that this woman was possibly more than just slightly eccentric, as he had thought the day before.

"I have forever," she said. She watched his transparent reactions and was honestly amused. "When I bought this house, I knew this was where I would be spending the rest of my life. Its very spirit has become part of me."

"But surely you don't have to injure yourself or take such risks," he said, casually assisting her in brushing the dust from her clothes. His mind took another leap as he touched her, but he maintained his friendly and nonchalant façade. "I'm sure we could find some local boys who would be glad for the work."

"No, I don't want to take a chance on having something ruined," she said. She brushed his hands away impatiently. "I don't want anyone else doing this. I use outside workmen only when absolutely necessary."

"But surely you haven't forgotten that I'm coming to help you," he said as he gave her an astonished look. "Remember? We agreed about that already."

As Amy came to her full senses after the confusion of the situation, she became aware of a sudden warmth that seemed to invade her in an insidiously infuriating way. It was a familiar yet alien feeling, and she deliberately turned away from young Harrison and wondered at her reaction. Picking up one of her fallen tools, postponed answering him.

"I mean, certainly the old boy himself in that

portrait in your bedroom would approve if I helped you," said Harrison with a slightly contrived laugh. "And you know there are tools and materials that can be used for this, some of them so advanced they could do this in a flash."

"That's just the thing," said Amy, fire coming into her eyes. "I'm trying to tell you that I need to do this myself, *in my own ancient way,* to be sure that I don't lose or destroy any valuable artifacts."

Harrison looked at her with his hands on his hips. "This is what you call carefully saving?" he asked.

She pushed his helping hand away when he reached to help her retrieve another tool, and seeing the anger sparking in her eyes, he immediately retreated. This wasn't the way to accomplish what he most desired. He understood that immediately. At the same time his mind went into overdrive. "Listen," he said as he lowered and softened his voice while massaging his chin, "I think I could design something that could X-ray and detect anything of value, and then maybe we could even go after it with a laser beam."

"What?" exclaimed Amy as she looked at him distastefully. "Bring X rays in here! Do you know how dangerous they are? Use lasers in this house. Never!"

She couldn't believe how irate such a thought made her. This house had been lovingly and carefully put together by the finest masons and carpenters, using their hands and basic tools. It had already been assaulted by cruel fate before she rescued it. It wasn't going to be ravished by that kind of outrage now.

Harrison was aghast as he watched her reaction. "For pete's sake, what's wrong with you?" he asked. "You just ripped this whole room apart and nearly killed yourself while you were doing it. What I'm talking about, if I can get it together in the right combination, would hardly touch a thing, and then you could very carefully remove only what absolutely had to be removed."

Amy looked at him and felt a bit contrite as she took in the mess around her and realized that a lot of good sound gypsum plaster had come down. Nevertheless the idea of ultramodern technology in this house was repugnant to her. "I told you last night I didn't want you coming in here with any wild ideas."

"But if you love this house the way you say you do, and you're restoring it for old Harrison the first down there, why not do it the simplest and easiest way? You know, I noticed several other places that are also being excavated around here, and those people are fully armed with the latest technology."

Amy looked at the floor and sighed. "Yes, I know what you mean," she said. "There's been an ongoing program for several years to save the old Victorian houses, and just a few months ago this whole village was proclaimed a national historical site. The place is packed with archaeological students, but they're still raking and dusting with their hands. Make no mistake about that."

"So I noticed," he said. He sat on the corner of a

41

sawhorse and then stood up when he noticed thick dust on his clothes. "That's what I was coming over to see you about. You know, as we were already discussing, I really want to spend my summer here, but with this archaeology thing and the people it's drawing, not to mention the usual summer folks who come here for the beach, every available room or apartment in town has been taken."

Amy looked at him silently, not really believing that he was going to suggest what she knew he was going to suggest. Suddenly she felt a constriction in her chest. The very thought took her breath away, yet at the same time there was a sort of push, a giddy acceptance that left her completely disconcerted.

"Anyway," she heard Harrison going on, "I guess I could get something over in Princess Anne. It's practically deserted in the summer, but that's nearly fifteen miles away, and I really want to spend my time in this house."

"So what are you saying?"

Amy looked at him in feigned perplexity, standing in the rays of dusty sunlight. She surveyed him with her hand on her hip. Taking a big breath, Harrison plunged on, even though now that he had begun, the idea seemed almost as ridiculous to him as it obviously did to her.

"I was thinking maybe you might rent me a room. I'd be right here, close by." He went on hastily, trying to ignore the perspiration that suddenly appeared along his collar. "I could give you the help you need and learn about my family at the same time."

Something in Amy urged her to accept, but at the same time she had never been so reluctant and outright flabbergasted. "You want *me,*" she said, "a person you just met yesterday, to let *you* come to live in *my* house *with* me!"

"No!" he answered, suddenly feeling ridiculous. "I mean, yes, that's what I want, but no, not the way you're making it sound. I said *rent* a room! You have plenty of rooms."

"But I just don't think that's the proper thing to do."

"Why not?" he asked, suddenly a little annoyed with her prudishness. "For crying out loud, we're practically relatives, so to speak. I mean, who more than me should be living in this house?"

"That's outrageous," said Amy, remembering the sad state of the house when she had bought it. "You certainly never did anything to preserve it!"

"Precisely," he said, trying not to sound as illogical as he knew his argument was. "I completely agree with what you're saying, but until yesterday I honestly had no way of knowing about this house or what had happened to it." He thought he saw her softening when he glanced into her eyes. He put on his most contrite and appealing face. "Truthfully, seeing that Bible yesterday and just experiencing everything you've done here makes me want to be a part of it, too."

Amy turned her head in incredulous amusement and met his eyes directly. "Do you think I'm stupid or something?"

"No," he said in real exasperation. "But what makes you think you're the only one who can have strong feelings about this place?"

The bluntness of his words seemed to have the magical effect he had been searching for. Amy turned away, the depth of her own emotions making her want to believe that someone else could feel as she did. Seeing his advantage, Harrison wasn't about to lose it.

"I did a little checking around," he said, speaking as softly and sincerely as he could. "I don't mean to inconvenience you. There's another street entrance on the back of the house, and you have rooms there that I could use just for the summer."

"But they're not—"

"They'll do," he insisted. "In fact, that's the first thing I'll do. I'll put enough work into them to make them habitable, and I'll pay for it myself in addition to rent. How's that for a deal?"

"But that's not necessary," she said, thinking of how filthy those rooms were. "There are rooms on this floor that are already completed."

"But you're so worried about propriety," he said, feeling nearly gleeful. He could almost sense his first victory, and that alone nearly created another disconcerting moment for him as he did his best to quell his physical response to her.

"Yes, of course," she said, "but this is the third floor, and as you said, rooms are scarce." A burst of inspiration had obviously touched her, too. "Maybe I could take in a few more roomers."

"Oh, but then you'd have them all over the

44

house, and there could be cooking and I don't know what all. I never meant anything like that."

"You're right," said Amy as the idea instantly fizzled. The very thought of such an invasion, not to mention what it might do to her antiques business, was unacceptable.

"No, seriously," he said, moving closer and giving her his most appealing look, "those rooms at the back would be fine."

"No, they are not," she said, suddenly impatient with him. "What on earth would Harrison the first have ever thought if one of his heirs were to stay in a place like that?"

"Oh, yes, what would he have thought?" said young Harrison in comic exaggeration.

"Cut it out," Amy said, moving toward the door. "I guess at least part of me is in the twentieth century, but I still can't help worrying about what people might say." She gave him a wry smile. "You shouldn't be denied the right to enjoy a bit of your heritage if you're really that interested." She gave him another gauging look and then seemed to make her decision. "Come with me."

She opened the door and led him down the long hallway to a highly polished mahogany door. It opened into a round tower of a room, which was richly paneled and masculine-looking. Windows encircled half of it, and in the middle stood a telescope. It could obviously be used to look out over the ocean or be tilted up toward the stars.

Young Harrison gasped in honest admiration. "Wow! This is marvelous."

"I thought you'd like it," she said, pleased with

his reaction. "I think it must have been the very private domain of the first Harrison."

"And you're telling me I can rent *this* room from you!"

"It seems only appropriate," she said with a smile. She found his reaction gratifying. "There's a private entry here as well." She walked to a small door. It opened out onto a small portico, and steps wound down all the way to the street. "I think Harrison the first would be very pleased to have you here."

As she spoke, Amy wondered what had got into her. This really was not a very wise thing to be doing, yet everything about it seemed right.

"I can't believe this," said Harrison V, struck by the charm of the circular room. There was a desk and a daybed that served as a couch as well. Everything was obviously of the same period as the house, yet was distinctly modern. Somehow he felt as if he could reach out from it and grasp the future. "This is absolutely wonderful." He shrugged. "What else can I say?"

Amy smiled. She felt wonderful. "Just promise you'll take good care of it," she said.

He nodded, and their eyes met.

Suddenly Amy found herself speechless as the warmth of the moment completely enveloped her. The windows seemed to form pictures waiting to be executed against the backdrop of the ocean, trees, and heavens, and she found herself looking into Harrison's eyes for ideas to complete them.

"Well," she said a little self-consciously. Dust fell

away from her as her hands hit her jeans. "I still have a lot of work to do. Maybe you'd better go on and make whatever arrangements you need to, and then I'll plan on seeing you?"

She looked at him questioningly.

"Oh, next week," he said hastily as he found himself involved with not only her eyes but various other areas of her anatomy. "By next week I'm sure I can have everything taken care of. Now what about the rent?"

"Oh, whatever the going rate is," she said, shrugging. "I don't know much about these things. I guess I can trust you, considering everything . . ."

Her voice trailed off, and Harrison felt a spark of protectiveness toward her. In a way she was being a little foolhardy. "Yes, I guess it's a good thing I've got the genes of old Harrison the first there to vouch for me. You can't get much more solid than the man who built this house, now can you?"

"You've got that right," she said, thankful for his adroit way of rescuing her from her inner fluster. "Now listen, though: I'm very serious about taking good care of everything. I'm a real fanatic about that."

Harrison V looked around the shining, immaculate room. "I can see that," he said. "You must work yourself to pieces in this place."

"I enjoy it," she said. "It seems like the right thing to do."

"Well, there's no denying that the atmosphere is great, but maybe I can make it a little easier for you."

47

She gave him a sharp look.

"I meant by giving you a hand now and then."

"Don't worry about it," she said as she escorted him from the room. She was moving carefully to avoid touching anything with her messy clothes. When they got to the bottom of the steps, she looked toward the kitchen. "I guess we can work out something with the meals," she said.

"Oh, you mean the table isn't always set for two then?" He looked in toward the dining room, where the table was bare now except for a center floral arrangement.

Amy colored and looked away as she remembered again how he had caught her in her frivolous fantasy the night before.

"No customers coming today?" he asked mischievously as he reached out and tipped up her chin.

"Obviously I'm not expecting anyone," she said breezily. Suddenly, as she stood there in her dirty, rumpled clothes in the midst of the shining house and as she squirmed under the ornery gaze of this man who reminded her so much of the one she adored in her dreams, she knew she had just made a terrible mistake in allowing him to come here to stay. What on earth had got into her?

"Listen," she said while she twisted away and tried to ignore the tingle of his touch. Too late she remembered the way he had left last evening. Somehow that departure had become mixed up with some of her other thoughts and fantasies, and now she knew she had to remedy the error she was

48

about to make. "Maybe this isn't such a good idea. Renting the room to you, I mean . . ."

"Are you telling me, an honest-to-God real-life Harrison James, that I can't trust your word?"

He had meant to be funny, hoping to jolly her out of her momentary reluctance, but Amy blanched and gave him a stricken look. "No, not at all," she said hesitantly. "It's just that all this is so unorthodox . . . I mean, one moment I'm in a room with plaster falling on my head and the next you're making arrangements to stay here. Perhaps I should think about this."

"All right," he said, suddenly chastened. "I guess I can understand that."

Seeing his face and manner, Amy immediately felt awful, and relented. "Well, only if you're absolutely sure there's no other place where you can stay . . ."

"I'll make very sure. I'll bring proof if necessary."

Amy smiled, an instant captive of his excessive antics, and gave up. "Okay," she said, "but this is strictly on a trial basis. I want you to understand that."

"Absolutely," he said with a grin. He reached out to touch her one more time. "But you've already made me feel I'm in a magical dream that's never going to end."

"Now I know you're nuts," she said with a nervous little laugh as she looked down at her filthy appearance. "But for the life of me, I'm not sure which one of us is the crazier, you or me!"

CHAPTER THREE

Harrison galloped down the porch steps two at a time. "Oh, by the way," he called, almost as an afterthought, "I'll be sending a few things down express. Is that all right?"

"Well, sure, I guess so," said Amy, suddenly not at all sure what she was agreeing to. Her voice trailed off as she looked away, more nervous than she had been in quite a while.

"Don't trouble yourself about them," he said. "I'll take care of everything as soon as I arrive. I'll call you and let you know what to expect."

Amy nodded and wondered again at her uncharacteristic impetuosity while she watched young Harrison go out the gate and get into his car. She had put hours and hours of work into that tower room, and in her dreams she had never imagined anyone except Harrison I in it. Now she had just cavalierly handed it over to a complete stranger. *Well, maybe not a total stranger,* she thought. She glanced up toward her bedroom and then impulsively went into the library, where she picked up the smaller portrait and looked pensively into the face of the real owner of her home.

A silly smile began to play over her face. *I guess I really won't mind,* she thought. *After all, he's a Harrison James, too.*

When she realized what a mess she was making with her dusty clothes, she rapidly retreated back upstairs to continue with her project.

Meanwhile, Harrison James V was ecstatic over his good fortune. He never would have believed he could have been so bold, but once the idea had struck him, to stay in that house just seemed the thing to do. Now he would have the whole summer to get to know Miss Amy Kyles in every way. His mind began to roam, and he knew he would soon be bursting with ideas. He couldn't wait to try out some of them in Amy's house. *Oh, excuse me,* he said to himself comically. *Harrison the first's house! By all means, let's get that straight!*

Two days later a parcel service truck pulled up outside Amy's house. To her surprise several large boxes were unloaded. She hadn't heard a word from Harrison V, so she was a little flabbergasted. The next day several more boxes arrived, and now Amy was more than a little put-out. Not knowing exactly what was inside the huge crates, she had no alternative but to leave them in the middle of her parlor. They were already causing problems with her antiques business. To say that she was a bit testy when Harrison finally called was a severe understatement.

"What in heaven's name is all this mess?" she shouted through the phone.

"It's my computer," he said offhandedly.

"Your . . . computer?"

"Yes. I need it to stay in touch with my work while I'm down there."

"Stay in touch!"

"Yes, through the phone, the way we're talking now. Using a modem, of course, that is until I—"

"Through the phone," she repeated inanely. "Modem?" Visions of some horrible modern monstrosity in her meticulously restored house nearly did her in. "You simply can't do something like that." She was holding her head and scowling as she looked at the sizes and number of the boxes. "It'll never fit in."

"We'll work it out," he said soothingly. "Trust me. You don't have anything to worry about."

"That's easy for you to say," she said bitingly. "You've already ruined at least one sale for me. You'd better get down here quick and take care of this."

"Just the words I wanted to hear," he said in a lecherous tone of voice. He wasn't the least bit intimidated. But he would not tell Amy what had been keeping him awake either, leaving him tired and irritable after a night of wrestling with his sheets and thinking about her in decidedly unpure ways.

"I'll give you until two o'clock tomorrow afternoon to get this mess out of here," she said firmly. "I told you I'd rent you a room, but I never told you that you could bring a computer into my house. And don't you even think of hooking it up to my telephone!"

"We'll talk about it when I get there," he said, and suddenly Amy had the weirdest feeling. She was outraged, but in spite of her very strong feelings, she sensed that she was somehow being overruled *in her own house.*

"There's nothing to talk about," she said. She shrugged the feeling away and hung up. She wasn't going to be manipulated like this. Who did he think he was anyway? A warm breath went across the back of her neck, and she compulsively looked toward the top of the stairs. Who indeed?

Harrison V held the phone receiver in his hand and listened to the buzz of the open line. His sureness had been more bravado than genuine confidence, but he instinctively felt this was the way to handle this vixen of a woman who was hiding behind such out-of-date, demure ways. He couldn't help wondering if he wasn't being a little presumptuous. But then he was struck by a happy feeling. He hung up the phone, stuck his hands in his pockets, and began to whistle as he walked away. "Nothing ventured, nothing gained," he said aloud as he thought of Amy undressed in the middle of that four-poster bed. He was sure that this woman demanded just the right touch of teasing, cavalier arrogance blended with a sweet gentleness, and he thought he knew exactly how to provide it, especially after he had read those Regency romance novels she was so enthralled with.

Moments after the telephone conversation Amy walked around the boxes warily and even gave one of them a little nudge with her foot. Surely all this couldn't be part of a computer. She pushed another box tentatively and gave it a reak kick this time. No. Obviously there were books and other things. Some of the boxes rattled. She was growing more distraught by the moment. Actually all she had to do was tell Harrison V that the deal was off, but that practicality seemed somehow distasteful to her. Bemused, she stood with one hand on her hip and the other to her head, staring at the boxes, and was startled when the doorbell ripped the silence.

A bit flustered, she went hurriedly to the door and greeted Lawrence Hartman, the head of the history department at UMES. "What a nice surprise," she said cordially as she tried to get her nervousness under control.

He smiled in warm anticipation. "I was out this way looking over all the historic site commotion and thought I'd drop by." A handsome, craggy man with the looks of a fortyish, slightly watered-down Gregory Peck, he stopped in his tracks. "What on earth is all this?"

"Oh," said Amy, completely nonplussed again. The elegant ambiance and warm charm of the parlor had been destroyed by the ugly boxes. "I agreed to rent a room to one of the descendants of the original owners of this house for the summer, and all this is his. I'm furious over the mess."

"Why would you do a thing like that?" Lawrence was solicitous.

Amy reddened and looked away. Lawrence was one of her favorite people, and they had been intellectual friends for a long time. "I don't know," she said before heaving a big sigh. "I think I'm beginning to get a little barmy."

"Oh, you're finally beginning to notice," he said

with a twinkle in his eyes. He retrieved a pipe from his pocket and lit it while Amy nervously hovered with an ashtray to catch his match and any other waste he might create. Walking around the boxes, he gave her an appraising look. "Well, I hope this doesn't mean you're going to make any drastic changes. Your work in this house has always been so fascinating."

"Oh, no," said Amy. She gave him a relieved smile and realized how glad she really was to see him. Suddenly everything seemed to be in perspective again. Motioning Lawrence toward the library, she went to the kitchen to get them some iced tea.

When she joined him again, he smiled. "You mentioned that you had just acquired another piece of Tang pottery when I talked with you the other day."

"Yes," she answered, her eyes bright with excitement. "A Bactrian horse, and it's absolutely wonderful."

She spent the next hour chatting and visiting with Lawrence while she showed him all her latest acquisitions, including a piece or two of Chippendale. It was just what she had needed, and she was effusive in her thanks to him for dropping by when he was ready to depart.

"Now you say one of the original owner's descendants is coming to stay?" He eyed the boxes again. "How on earth did that come about?"

"It's a long story," she said with a little laugh. "Remember the Bible I found?"

"Oh, yes," he said. "So you went through with your plan then?"

"Yes. And it's absolutely extraordinary. You wouldn't believe how much this young Harrison James resembles the original Harrison James."

"Really," said Lawrence as he gave her another gauging look. "Same name, too. Interesting. Well, I'll be looking forward to meeting this *reincarnation,*" he added with an indulgent smile. "I should have known you'd never stand for something so simple as a ghost in the house. You'd have to have the real thing."

"Why not?" she said, enjoying the indulgent camaraderie that had always been a part of their relationship. "Watch out now that you don't get ashes on my porch."

Lawrence rolled his eyes playfully and tapped his pipe out carefully on the ground. "Wouldn't think of it," he said, and gave her a smile tinged with both humor and respect.

"We'll have dinner," she said as he went down the steps. "I'll call you when everything is sorted out."

"I'll plan on it," he called with a final wave.

Amy was very pleased and felt happy as she walked back into the parlor. The boxes were definitely a mess, but it would work out. As she thought of young Harrison V and his wild ideas and also thought of the original Harrison in the portrait upstairs, she had a funny feeling that there was more than one missing link in the chain that connected the two of them.

Nevertheless, she felt much better. The thought

of seeing young Harrison again was decidedly pleasant. But when she gave the boxes another glance and remembered what was in them, she made up her mind to have a definite understanding about this sort of thing before it got out of hand.

She was ready, her most resolute look in place, when Harrison V arrived the next day. His car was laden down with more boxes and paraphernalia that Amy couldn't identify. One scruffy-looking suitcase was the only thing that seemed to have anything to do with clothing.

"Now just a moment," she said as, laden down with boxes, he started up the porch steps. "Before you come in here with another thing, we have to get something straight!"

"Such as?" he said, going on past her and struggling with the screen door while Amy stood by.

"Such as where you are going to put this contraption," she said as she waved at the boxes. "I can't have something like that in this house. Everyone who comes in here expects to find things that are historical."

"This will be historical," he said with an exaggerated lift of his brows. "When I get through with the experiment I'm going to perform on it, it will definitely have become another stepping-stone in the annals of history."

"I don't think so," she said firmly.

He stopped and looked at her appraisingly. "Well, I have to do my work," he said softly. "I may have the summer off, but someone like me never stops." He looked for an analogy that would appease her. "It's like being a writer or an artist. When we're inspired, we have to work."

She looked at him dubiously.

"Look," he said as he came over and took her by the arms, "this house has done crazy things to me. I can't tell you what it is, but it's almost as if the simplicity of the beginnings of so many of the things that are now complicated is somehow giving me a new understanding of my work. I have ideas that are just incredible."

"Well, then go back to your lab and work on them," she said coldly. "You can't come in here and mess up my house. I won't permit it."

"But that's just the thing," he said as suddenly the atmosphere surrounding them seemed to change. He had the urge to hold her and caress her, and he just knew Amy felt the same way toward him. She thought of a tiny, fluffy kitten rolling in her arms and had the strangest urge to seek that sensation in the embrace of this man. His lips were just inches away from hers as their eyes met. "It's you and this house," he whispered as he pulled her close, the victim of an intense magnetism.

For one fleeting moment their lips met, and then Amy jumped away. "Cut it out," she said, and looked at him aggrievedly. She was truly angry at her own reaction as well, knowing she wanted him to continue.

"I'm sorry," he said, honestly contrite. But then the look in her eyes drove him wild. "No, I'm not. I've dreamed about this."

"But this is insane!" she cried. "Now you just pack up your junk and get out of here!"

"You told me I could stay here," he said insistently. "You made a deal."

Something about the authority in his voice seemed to pull a string in Amy. She looked at him and couldn't believe her own wild reactions as he pulled her close again, this time gently and tentatively, and kissed her with fire and passion. Within seconds she was a captive of her own desires and had no way of defending herself as he held her in an embrace that left her feeling weak and fragile. It was only the crashing of boxes and loud rapping on the door which saved her.

"Amy, Miss Kyles . . ."

She pulled away roughly and gave Harrison an infuriated look. "Arthur," she said in a slightly trembling voice as she went to the door. "I'm glad you came."

She rapidly straightened her clothes and looked at Harrison warningly. "The well is in the backyard, Arthur, and I'll be with you in just a moment. I'm hoping you'll be able to clean it and make it usable again."

Harrison V gave her a contrite look and raged at himself for his lack of control. This was definitely not the way he had planned to carry out his seduction. Now he could tell he was going to have to mend a lot of fences, but as Amy went past him with a haughty air, he knew that the softness and eagerness of those lips were just as real as the ardor he had experienced the other night. Obviously his dreams and fantasies had barely hinted at what was really there.

Mustering all his courage and fortitude, he went resolutely about bringing in the rest of his belongings while Amy went on with her negotiations with Arthur. Fortunately she had a rather lengthy conversation with the well man, so Harrison began taking his things upstairs to the room that was to be his.

"What do you think you're doing?" she asked as the kitchen door slammed and she came back into the parlor. Harrison was juggling several boxes while he tried to move awkwardly up the stairs.

"Moving in," he said, giving her a quick glance and a conciliatory smile.

"You can't be serious! After what just happened here I can't allow that!"

"You have to," he said, meeting her eyes boldly and directly. "It's all arranged."

"Well, just unarrange it," she said. Her eyes flashed, and she assumed her most haughty stance. "This is completely outrageous, and you know it."

Carefully he set his packages down, making sure they wouldn't fall down the steps. Slowly and deliberately he came down the stairs, his eyes never leaving hers while he brushed his clothes with his hands. Amy was speechless, almost transfixed as he moved directly toward her. Never wavering, he reached for her hand, and she gasped. Before she could pull away, he touched his lips to her hand and searched her eyes. "I'm sorry," he said as he willed her to understand. "I shouldn't have taken advantage of you."

Amy was completely defenseless as he adroitly implemented his strategy. His sincerity appealed tremendously to her, reminding her of her fantasies, and she found herself relenting almost instantaneously. "No, you shouldn't have," she said weakly.

"It won't happen again," he said as he continued to hold her eyes with his own.

She blanched and looked away.

"Unless you want it to."

She looked back sharply and felt the fire of outrage again. Then she remembered the incredible softness and sweetness that had accompanied the earlier passionate rage. Amid the heady fragrances of summer and the scintillating scent of the house and all its mystery, she suddenly wanted more, much more. But at last her common sense won out. "I don't think this is very appropriate."

A tiny muscle clenched in his jaw. "I'm staying," he said firmly. "We made an agreement, and we're both going to stick to it."

Her mouth opened, but she was speechless. For the life of her she couldn't find the words or the ability to shout him out of her house and her life. He gave her one more appraising look and then turned to resume his tasks.

Amy was flabbergasted as she stood by ineffectually. She couldn't believe she was allowing this to happen, but she felt incapable of stopping it.

"Now about the computer," he said.

That brought her to.

"Oh, no," she said, raising her hand. "Now that definitely is something that I won't have."

"It won't be any problem at all," he said placatingly.

But Amy was caught up in the complete inanity of her predicament. *I won't allow a computer in the house*, she thought, *but I'm allowing a man who just took advantage of me to move into my house!* A prickle went up her spine, and she felt a peculiar compulsion. She couldn't believe this, but letting him move into her house still seemed to be all right in some strange way. Nothing inside her told her there was anything wrong with it. She, incredibly, had no sense of indiscretion. On the contrary, it was almost as if she were following some prescription of fate.

"Are you listening to me?" asked Harrison while Amy tried to fathom the meaning of her feelings.

"N-no, what?" she stammered.

He looked at her and for just a moment wondered at his sanity. What had gotten into him? This woman was different from anyone he'd ever known and so eccentric that it was almost ridiculous, yet he felt a compulsion to win her. He nearly relented, but then he remembered his one driving desire. Just the thought of that body naked in his arms was all that he needed.

"I was saying," he said patiently, "that the entire computer can be easily camouflaged in the big cupboard that you have there near the phone."

She looked at him incredulously. "That *big cupboard,*" she said with outraged emphasis, "is a genuine signed John Needles desk. I couldn't possibly allow you to compromise its integrity with such a monstrosity, and I've already told you to leave my telephone out of this!"

"Now just hold on," he said while he wondered anew at his attraction to this bizarre and intransigent woman. "You must have a television set in this house."

She looked at him warily and lifted her chin in stubbornness.

"Don't tell me you don't watch TV."

He looked around and tried to spot where it might be. "Let me see," he said, trying to remember every room in the house. With a sure instinct he headed for the library. "Aha!" he shouted after he had opened several doors and found what he was looking for. "Is this *whatever it is* compromised by this modern vice?" He stood triumphantly, and Amy glared at him.

"That's entirely different," she said.

"I hardly think so," he said somewhat smugly. "And I daresay a further examination would probably find another television in the bedroom, hiding inside another antique cupboard."

"All right," she said, and gave him a venomous look. "But you seem to be forgetting something. This is my house!"

"Oh, no," he said, dropping his voice conspiratorially. "I could never forget that. But you made a deal with me."

"Not to let you have the run of the place," she said emphatically. "This is really just too much. If people come into that parlor expecting to find good-quality authentic antiques, I can't have them opening the door to one and finding a computer!"

63

"So lock the doors. Who's to know?"

"You can't do things like that," she said in disgust. "When people pay hundreds or even thousands of dollars for something, they want to look it over."

"So I'll figure something out," he said nonchalantly. "It won't hurt anything until I at least get a phone up to my room, will it?"

"There aren't any jacks up there, and I'm not sure I want lines along those walls."

For a second they stood and glared at each other in an apparent standoff. Then Harrison began to smile. "Okay," he said. "So how much is it?"

Amy looked at him, clearly perplexed. "What do you mean?"

He gave her another impatient look. "You said that's a genuine signed John something or other. How much is it? I'll buy it, and then it won't matter if my computer is inside it."

"You are out of your mind," she said in complete amazement. "That's about the craziest thing I've ever heard."

"Do you quibble like this with all your paying customers?" He smiled and relished the flustered look that came over her face. He again felt that now-familiar physical response to her.

"Three thousand dollars," she said in outright challenge.

"Sold," he said unflinchingly. "Will you take a check?"

"But you can t . . That's ridiculous," she said exasperatedly.

"I don't want to argue about it," he said, and gave her that direct, intimidating gaze again.

"Oh, put the stupid thing in it and shut up," she said, finally giving in and admitting defeat.

"Just as soon as I pay for it," he said. He walked to the desk and casually looked it over. "Sure hope I'm getting a good deal."

She looked away more annoyed than she would ever have imagined she could be. "I'm an honest businesswoman," she said with a steely tinge to her voice.

"Good. Then just be sure you tell everyone that this belongs to me," he said with a satisfied smirk. "And don't let anyone touch it."

It was hours before Amy calmed down enough to realize the implications of those few moments with Harrison V. He nonchalantly had gone on and moved in all his belongings and then breezily installed his small compact computer system into the John Needles desk, making it an effective console. Harrison was delighted with his new acquisition, which had the lid that dropped down into a wide work area and all sorts of compartments and drawers for his papers and disks. He was soon busily putting it to use while she went into the library and seethed.

I don't believe you're letting this happen, she said sullenly to herself. Yet she was. There was no doubt about it. She looked at the check that lay on the table next to her. It was almost as if he were turning her into an outsider in her own house. That was what finally brought her to her senses. If he was going to be here, then they at least had to be cordial. *And we're going to have an understanding*, she thought determinedly. This time she wasn't going to be put off.

"Harrison," she said coolly, walking into the parlor.

"Yes," he said, obviously immersed in what he was doing.

Amy looked at the small green and white screen on the computer and wondered what on earth could possibly be so fascinating about something that looked so cold and sterile.

"We have to talk."

"I thought we'd already done that."

"You know what I mean," she said. "All of this is terribly unorthodox and irregular."

"Oh, really?" he said. He felt his face beginning to pucker, and he had to struggle to keep from mimicking her by adding, "How quaint." But he could see that she had softened, and the bluff that he had gambled on to balance out his earlier impetuosity seemed to have worked.

She motioned toward the library.

He smiled at her and followed.

"I can't imagine why I haven't thrown you out," she said, using her sternest voice.

He looked at her, waiting for her to go on.

She took a big breath and searched for just the right words. "Now about this afternoon—"

"Let's forget about this afternoon," he said as he shattered the gloom with his brightest smile. "I was a smart aleck, and you have every right to be angry with me—"

66

"Please hear me out," she said. "You requested a room from me on a strictly business basis."

"Let's just leave it be," he said softly.

She looked at him and suddenly felt a melting that she couldn't deny.

"We have a lot of things to learn about each other." He went on as he arose and moved closer to her. "I don't know why I have such crazy feelings when I come around here, but you know somehow this is the way it is supposed to be."

"That's silly."

"It's not silly," he said.

The room seemed to glow around them, and suddenly Amy felt a wonderful sense of kinship and understanding. "I don't know what to say." She agonized, trying to find the words.

"Don't say anything."

He reached up and gently caressed her lips, softly, demandingly. "This is called chemistry," he said. "It's something we don't have any control over."

Confused, Amy reached out to him and felt the simple joy of his arms around her when she responded to his gentle caresses.

"I can't thank you enough for agreeing to allow me to stay," he said, pushing her hair back and tracing the damp strands that surrounded her face. "I can't tell you how sweet you are to do such a thing."

Amy had showered and changed into a silky kimono, and now she looked like a splendid Chinese jewel. She lay back and gazed into Harrison's eyes, and for a moment he seemed to embody her every fantasy.

"Oh, hold me," she whispered as she gave into her need. "Hold me and never let me go."

CHAPTER FOUR

Young Harrison could hardly believe his ears as he pulled Amy closer in response to her breathless demands. His lips traveled over her with sweet urgency, and for a moment he was sure all his fondest dreams were about to come true. Then, in a moment of piercing insight, he knew Amy wasn't responding to him, at least not to him alone. "Amy?" he asked as he pushed her hair back and tenderly scanned her face.

"Yes," she said, opening her eyes to meet his. Her expression was one of passion and deep desire as she invited his lips to her own again and offered a sweet promise of greater delights still to come.

Unable to resist, Harrison tightened his embrace. Her body fitted the niches of his own in the perfect way that nature must have envisioned when the magic of love was created. Thinking now his earlier perception was little more than a slight case of anticipatory jitters, he gave in to his emotions and kissed and caressed her with increasing ardor. His lips left hot trails on her neck and moved sensually lower while his hands began to make some definite demands.

"Harrison," said Amy in a faraway, whispery voice. But just as the words "I've dreamed of the happiness you could bring me" flitted through her mind, she realized that once again she had allowed fantasy to infringe on reality.

Harrison immediately sensed the change, for her body stiffened. She pulled away and looked at him in wild despair. "Oh, dear me," she said as her hand moved unconsciously to calm her heaving bosom. "What must you think of me?"

Harrison could barely keep from laughing. The very melodrama of her pose was almost more than he could believe, and he tried valiantly to control his trembling lips and dancing eyes. "I think I'd like to go on with this," he said mischievously.

But before he could continue, Amy pushed him away and turned swiftly. She marched a safe distance away and met his amused eyes in fiery confusion. "This mustn't happen again," she said sternly. "It just mustn't."

Harrison looked at her and then began to laugh. "Why not?" he asked. "You were enjoying it just as much as I was."

"Please," she said, holding her hand up in admonition. She was scarlet and refused to meet his eyes again. "Don't make me do something we both might regret."

Realizing he had probably gone about as far as he dared, Harrison gave her another gauging look. "Yes, of course," he said with a twinkle in his eye. "We wouldn't want that now, would we?"

"Make sure you understand it," she said, then swept past him and out of the room.

And just who are you trying to kid? Harrison mused. *And for that matter what's come over you?* he asked himself as again he wondered how he could possibly have become so wildly attracted to such an obviously erratic woman. But then the warmth of that flesh and the visions of those breasts swelling in passion, waiting for the touch of his willing hands, told him the answer.

But Amy was truly embarrassed now and wondered how she would ever extricate herself from this ridiculous situation with her dignity intact. She went straight to her room, where she walked around nervously. *You must go down and insist that he leave at once,* she ranted to herself. *You must!*

She pulled down the covers on her bed viciously and looked up at the portrait of Harrison I with real malice. Would she ever have the courage to confront Harrison V again? His dancing eyes had followed her all the way up the stairs. She had made a big enough fool of herself for one day. It could wait until tomorrow, and then she would decide what to do.

With that settled, she chanced another glance at the portrait of Harrison I. For just a second it gave her a feeling of security before she looked away in a huff. *Oh, you are ridiculous,* she said to herself.

Somehow, though, Amy and young Harrison managed to avoid each other for the next few days. It was as though Harrison intuitively understood that he needed to lie low and bide his time. Busy with the continuing restoration of her house and the antiques business and with her outside

71

interest in the historical site projects, she was also involved in the Somerset Historical Society and the restoration of a Scottish manor house in Princess Anne called Teackle Mansion. Amy seemed to miss Harrison whenever he was about. And as the days went by, somehow the magnitude of the embarrassing incident, as she had labeled it to herself, seemed to diminish.

Harrison, for the most part, was extremely busy, too. Once he had settled into the tower room, he set up yet another small experimental computer there and began to make plans for the complete computerization of the entire house, which would virtually eliminate many of the arduous and monotonous tasks that Amy performed daily. It was a simple question of a few ingenious and generally unnoticeable mechanical adjustments here and there and the filling of several floppy disks with his own brand of genius.

"You see," he explained to Amy when they finally settled down enough to talk to each other. "The computer is just another machine. It depends entirely upon the human mind to make it function. That ultimately also means its possibilities are limitless."

Amy looked at him with a touch of bewilderment while he went on. It was almost as if they both were mutually appreciative of such a nice safe subject. As he talked while making adjustments to the computer that Amy didn't in any way understand, she felt herself relax in an easy way.

"So you see," Harrison was going on, "the big deal now is not to communicate through the telephone or through the keyboard, but to program the hardware so that it actually can sense brain waves."

"What?" said Amy, suddenly feeling nervous. "You're talking about this thing's reading minds or something?"

"No, no, no." He laughed. "I'm talking about being able to give commands and run programs just by thinking. Of course, it will be an individualized thing."

Amy looked at him incredulously as she noticed for the first time several small dark patches which Harrison had attached near his ear and forehead. "You're serious," she said as she stepped back. "You're going to plug yourself into that thing."

The expression on her face was just too rich. Harrison began to laugh in great bellows. "I guess you could put it that way," he said as he reached into his back pocket for his handkerchief. Wiping tears of merriment away, he started to explain more. "You see—"

"No, I don't want to hear about this," said Amy. The sight of all this on the antique desk was almost the final indignity. "I'll bet John Needles is turning over in his grave," she said as she ran her hands over the old wood.

"I'll bet not," said Harrison with relish. "I'd say from the way this desk is organized he was a man who was obviously trying to make things better in his own time. And in the meantime, if I pull this off, he'll have become part of history again."

"Spare me," said Amy as she felt herself reacting to his ever-optimistic and zany humor again. But she couldn't help smiling when she noted how the electrodes he'd attached to himself had mussed his hair. He looked like a mischievous little boy grown up. Yet she had to admit there was a definite aura of nonchalant sexy magnetism about him, too, as she once again felt the beginning of that warm response from deep within her.

Smiling, he went back to work and gave a little shrug. Almost unconsciously he began to pound his hands in a staccato way as some sort of rhythm seemed to flow through him, punctuated by a verbal *ompah, pah*. His entire body contorted in a funny way.

"Oh, my God," said Amy, who reached out to him.

His eyes were glassy with joy, and he smiled and examined some small wires.

"Harrison!" exclaimed Amy, filling with panic. She reached unthinkingly for the electrodes.

"What?" he said as he looked up, startled.

"You're being electrocuted!" she shouted. "Turn it off."

She looked frantically for the plug, and Harrison began to laugh as he participated in yet another rhythmic motion. "No, I'm not," he said. "I've set this up so I can also listen to my favorite jazz records without disturbing anyone else."

"Jazz records," said Amy in dead pan. "You're listening to a stereo?"

"Something like that," he said. "Isn't it great? Civilized, too. You didn't hear a thing, did you?"

"No," she said as she shook her head. "But you

certainly are a sight to behold. Isn't this something you could do in your own room?"

"Yes," he said excitedly. "That's what I'm going to try next. I'm going upstairs and see if I can activate this computer down here with my mind from up there."

"Oh, my God," said Amy. "We can't have this."

But she was talking to herself. Harrison had bounded out of the room and up the steps.

"Harrison?" called Amy, following him up the stairs. "You can't be serious about this."

"Sure am," he answered as she came to his door. "And listen. Remember the discussion we had about ice cream on the first day when I visited you?"

"Ice cream?" said Amy. This whole thing was rapidly becoming like an old Marx Brothers movie.

"Go down and look in the kitchen," he said. "When I finish here, I'll come down and show you how it works."

"My kitchen?" asked Amy suspiciously. "You've done something to my kitchen?"

"No," he said a bit impatiently. "I made you an ice-cream freezer." His eyes began to dance again, and Amy turned to go, feeling she had missed something that was vital to the understanding of this whole situation. "On your way," he said, "stop and tell me what you see on the screen of the computer down there."

"You are too much," said Amy as she realized how he was ordering her around but Harrison didn't seem to notice.

75

She made a hasty retreat and started resignedly down the stairs. Although she had promised herself that she wouldn't do it, she couldn't help going over to the John Needles desk and the computer sitting there. Pulled toward it, almost as if she were a magnet responding to metal, she flushed deeper yet and then began to laugh. The monitor read, "You are exceptionally beautiful today, Miss Amy. Would you be good enough to have an ice-cream sundae with me later tonight?"

"Oh, I don't believe this," said Amy, raising her hand to her head and looking around the room. How could something like this be happening in her exquisite nineteenth-century haven?

"Answer, please." The monitor blinked at her insistently.

"I will not," said Amy with a touch of huff.

"Type your answer, please," the monitor spelled out.

"Why, of all the impertinence," said Amy. Her hand came to her breast, and suddenly it was almost as if the machine had taken on a life of its own. She stood silent while it continued to blink, almost as if the screen had become a face and the words, eyes. She found herself beginning to reach out tentatively. It was as if she were transfixed. Her fingers trembled as she touched the keys softly.

"Thank you very much. I'd love to," she typed onto the screen.

"All right!" came the instantaneous reply. "See you about eight."

"You're crazy," said Amy as she began to laugh.

But she wasn't sure whom she was talking to: herself or Harrison or the computer. Never in her life had she imagined that she would be doing anything like this. She turned and walked toward the kitchen.

The encounter with the ice-cream freezer was no less funny or traumatic. As Amy stood before it, she was completely mystified. It looked like any normal turn-of-the-century machine. Just as she was about to label it a joke Harrison came bounding into the kitchen.

"Can you believe that?" he asked excitedly.

"Believe what?" said Amy, looking away from the freezer.

"The computer down here picked up directly from my brain waves. I didn't type in a thing."

"You didn't?" said Amy numbly. She knew so little about these things that the significance of what he was saying was lost on her.

He looked at her a bit disappointedly.

"I told you I don't know anything about these things." Amy suddenly felt both sorry and inadequate.

Seeing her expression, Harrison came quickly to the rescue. "Ah, well, not to worry," he said breezily. "You will in time. In the meantime, it's the results that count. Now the challenge is to extend out until I can reach my colleagues in my MIT lab in the same manner."

"This really sounds terribly ominous to me," said Amy, who again gave him a wary look.

"Not at all," he said firmly. "Now about this little baby . . ."

Amy's attention returned to the ice-cream freezer as Harrison's face came alive again.

"All we need to make it work is an ice-cream recipe. I've already loaded it with the basic ingredients to make authentic ice cream. All you have to decide is what kind you want."

"But where are the—"

Amy was perplexed as she began to examine the gadget more carefully. She felt nothing cold and had no idea where the ingredients might be. Although it looked like an old freezer and the wood was real, the rest seemed alien to her.

"Don't worry about it," he said smugly. "Just give me one of your favorite recipes and watch."

Again wondering why she was doing this, Amy obediently produced a recipe from her file.

Harrison couldn't resist a teasing touch as their fingers lightly collided, and Amy looked quickly away. Smiling broadly, he once again took in the ripe innocence of her face and demeanor and cautioned himself about the need for patience. After the other evening, with the effects of that last romantic encounter still indelibly marked on his mind, Harrison had unconsciously resolved to do whatever it took to reach her, knowing the ultimate reward would be more than worth the effort.

Watching him to be sure he did nothing to damage her recipe, which itself was a genuine collector's item, Amy was more than a little dubious when Harrison sent his hand over the top of the machine in a precise motion that resembled something a magician might do. To her amazement a small light appeared on a tiny mechanical arm.

Harrison carefully scanned the recipe with it and then motioned the arm back into place.

"Who are you trying to kid?" asked Amy, beginning to think this was some childish trick.

"No one," he said excitedly. "Just watch."

To Amy's amazement, the machine suddenly seemed to come to life. Small clicks and other sounds she couldn't identify preceded a soft, whirring sound.

"Your ice cream is ready," said a tinny voice. "Would you care for topping?"

Amy's face was a picture to behold, and Harrison laughed jubilantly. "Answer it," he said.

"You answer it," she replied as the enormousness of all of this began to sink in. "I think I've talked to enough machines for one day."

"Hold the toppings until further notice," said Harrison, watching her coyly. "Hold serving until eight P.M."

Amy looked at him questioningly.

"Remember?" he said. "We're having ice-cream sundaes then."

"Oh, yes," said Amy as she sat down. "How could I forget?"

Suddenly she felt very old and very sad. It was as if everything that she had tried valiantly to preserve and hold in one place in time were suddenly being compromised. She didn't like these intrusive electronic things in her life, and she almost felt like crying.

Harrison became alarmed. "Why the sad look?" he asked as he came over to her.

"I don't like these things in my house," she said

flatly. "They aren't what Harrison the first would have had."

"Aren't you going a little far with that?" he demanded with more than a little impatience. "Do you enjoy being some kind of slave or something? To a ghost yet, for God's sake?"

"No, of course not," said Amy as she realized how ridiculous she must have sounded. Flushing, she tried to find more appropriate words. "It's just a quality that I'm talking about. A grace, something I can't equate with things like that." She waved unceremoniously toward the ice-cream freezer.

"Is that so?" he said. "Does this look like a real antique or not?" He thumped the ice-cream maker resoundingly.

"Well, yes, but—"

"And . . ." he said hesitantly before he began to move about the room. He dashed to the dining room. Amy heard the china cabinet door open. Dishes clinked, and she winced. Returning with some of her best dessert bowls, he walked back to the freezer. "Cancel previous serving instructions," he said after another magical wave. "Serve immediately."

Within moments implements had appeared and disappeared back into the recesses and two dishes had been filled with ice cream. "Is that real old-fashioned maple walnut ice cream, just the way Grandma used to make it, or not?"

Amy couldn't stop herself from putting it to the test. Taking the silver spoon he produced, she looked into Harrison's eyes as the first taste melted

80

in her mouth. Pleasure filled her face, and she looked at him in amazement.

"Is that good, or isn't it?" he asked softly.

"It's wonderful," she responded in complete capitulation. "Absolutely incredible."

"And you didn't kill yourself to produce it," he said. "You're sitting here in your authentic antique house, eating authentic antique ice cream, and you have plenty of time to go and work on your dissertation or any other thing that might use your mind far more productively."

"But there's something about the satisfaction of doing some of those things—"

"You're deluding yourself," he said. "Now if you'll just let me, I can do some really marvelous things for you. You'd never have to dust again or—"

"Oh, now please," she said, and gulped another spoonful of the ice cream. "Ice cream is one thing, but let's not get carried away."

"No problem," he said. "If you don't like what I do, it's a simple matter of removing the program disk, and that's the end of it."

Amy looked at him doubtfully, not even quite sure she knew what a program disk was or how one went about removing it.

"Should I trash the plans for the ice-cream maker?" he asked softly.

Her mouth was full of the creamy delight as she gave him a conciliatory smile. "No," she said, and spooned in yet another bite. "But just make sure you don't do anything to tear up the house."

"Speaking of which," he said, moving a little

81

closer to her, "the laser–X-ray thing is really coming together, too."

"Eat your ice cream," she said, and began to laugh. "It's starting to melt." His face was so intense with boyish delight and enthusiasm that she almost felt like a mother lovingly admonishing her child.

"So it is," he said with a hint of sheepishness.

A glow seemed to surround them as they sat in the enormous room in their own little emotional cocoon. Harrison knew he had never felt so fine or content in his life while Amy felt the warmness and happiness of childhood happily merge into the satisfaction of a sweet, successful today.

Slowly he reached out to her. Setting his ice-cream dish aside, he moved closer. His eyes met hers, and they both felt the warm communion that was beginning to bind them together. In a spontaneous, almost childlike gesture he took the spoon from her hand and filled it again with ice cream. Harrison and Amy both gloried in the passion that was mirrored in the deep pools of their eyes. She opened her mouth leisurely and accepted the wonderful delicacy from the spoon. With great satisfaction Harrison watched her lips move in sensual slow motion and then refilled the spoon and gave himself a sample of the ice cream. Reveling in its creamy texture as it rolled around his mouth, he offered yet another taste to her. They didn't speak, for they were entirely caught up in this moment of very sensual sharing.

As they finished the dessert, Harrison set the dishes aside and reached for Amy's hands. His

heart was pounding with the intensity of his emotion while her moist lips moved with supreme satisfaction. "May I kiss you, Miss Amy Kyles?" he
asked as he moved closer. Not waiting for an answer, his mouth met hers in a sweet savagery, and
soon the delicious flavors of the ice cream were
mixed with the heat of their passion.

Feeling as though she were being swept away in
an ethereal out-of-body experience, Amy gave in
to the sweet oblivion that threatened to overtake
her completely. Filled with a strange euphoria,
she kissed Harrison back, meeting his lips and
tongue with passionate thrusts, while she reveled
in the feeling of being crushed against his body.

"Harrison . . ." she murmured. "Harrison
. . ."

Again Harrison had the odd feeling that it was
not really his name that Amy was moaning and he
drew away. "Amy?" He gave her a puzzled look.

Flushing, Amy pulled away, too.

Somehow the spirit of Amy Kyles, the modern
twentieth-century woman, emerged to save the
situation. There would be no shrinking-violet hysterics this time. "Well, I trust," she said with just a
touch of shy breathlessness, "that that thanks you
properly for the ice cream."

Fascinated anew, Harrison gave her a long and
slow perusal, again enjoying her ripe, flushed appearance and the spirit in her eyes. "Maybe,
maybe not," he said slyly.

His eyes danced with merriment behind his
dark-framed glasses, and for just a moment Amy
could almost visualize him in the portrait upstairs,

especially as if he had just told a particularly naughty anecdote.

"Well, it will have to do," she said archly. "I have other things to take care of now."

"I doubt that," he said. He raised his eyebrows questioningly at Amy, who smiled at him.

She walked away with exaggerated dignity, moving toward the parlor, only to catch herself at the huge wooden sliding doors that opened into the foyer. She turned and called out to him, "And don't forget to put the dishes back in the cupboard after you've washed them."

Harrison stopped still in amazement and then began to laugh. "Sure thing," he called out. "Whatever makes you happy."

With a jaunty little step he scooped up the dishes and walked to the sink. Suddenly he stopped in mid-stride as yet another idea for a new invention came to him. Moments later he was upstairs in his room, working busily at his drafting board.

Meanwhile, Amy went back to her own projects, noting that the humid heat of summer was rapidly descending on both her house and the town in general. When the doorbell rang, she remembered that Mrs. Donkenny was coming by to see the Aaron Willard clock Amy had recently acquired. Blushing because she was dressed casually in skimpy summer clothes and had nearly forgotten the appointment, Amy went breathlessly to the door.

"Come in, come in," she said to the older woman, who was extremely wealthy and was one of Amy's best customers. "How are things in Princess Anne?"

"Quiet," said the woman meaningfully, and Amy recalled how different that town was from Culbert's Cove in the summer. "I've just come from the Teackle Mansion. You know, when I think of how that manor was vandalized by being turned into apartments for so many years I could just die."

"I know," said Amy solicitously. "There seems to have been so little appreciation for the finer things—"

But she stopped in the middle of her sentence when Mrs. Donkenny came upon the computer on the John Needles desk. Amy could almost see hair bristling and hackles rising on the woman's back. "What is this?" Mrs. Donkenny asked in outrage.

"It belongs to the man who bought the desk," said Amy hastily. "He—he's just using it, or I mean, leaving it there for a few days—"

"You would allow this fine piece of furniture to be compromised in such a way!"

For a second Amy almost smiled as she realized how fanatically ridiculous the woman sounded.

"He bought it. I guess he can use it in any way he sees fit," said Amy, beginning to speak rapidly and trying to guide the woman away. "Actually you'd probably find the whole thing very interesting. You see, he's a descendant of the original owner of this house, and he's staying here this summer—"

"Here, in this house with you?" the woman sniffed.

"He's renting a room," said Amy, but she flinched inwardly.

"My word, you aren't thinking of turning *this* house into apartments, are you?" Mrs. Donkenny's face filled with distaste.

"No, of course not," said Amy. "In fact, he's almost as interested in the research and restoration of this house as I am." She felt uneasy again as she realized how she was stretching the truth and why.

"Using the computer, no doubt, to facilitate it," said the woman peevishly. "My heavens, I don't think anything is sacred so far as those things are concerned these days."

"They're really just another tool," said Amy in weak defense. But she could see that Mrs. Donkenny was completely out of sorts now. It was obvious that the whole visit would prove futile, for suddenly Amy had the feeling that everything about the house had become suspect to Mrs. Donkenny.

After the stuffy woman had declined to buy the clock and left, Amy walked back to the computer on the desk. Suddenly she had decidedly malevolent feelings about it and everything it stood for. She had just lost a very big sale, and she knew it. Clenching her fists, she turned and walked toward the stairs.

She was in full fury by the time she reached the top floor and knocked angrily on Harrison's door. "I told you about leaving that computer out down there," she said as she looked into his surprised face.

"Oh, yes, I'm sorry," he said. "I guess I forgot."

"Well, your forgetting just cost me a fat sale," she said angrily. "And I won't have any more of this!"

"Oh, you won't?" he said, an amused expression on his face. "Just the way you'd have no more ice cream, I suppose."

That did it. Amy for the first time realized the ramifications of their intimate encounter of just a short time before. "Do something about it, and do it now," she said through clenched teeth. "If you cause me any more problems, you're going to have to leave."

"Okay," he said in instant submission. "I'll go down and close it up right now."

But his eyes said other things when he watched her stride away in angry hauteur. And he wasted no time in returning to the project he was working on. *Not just yet, little lady,* he said to himself. *I'm not going to leave just yet.*

CHAPTER FIVE

The next morning both Amy and Harrison felt uncomfortable, but soon their good natures and basic common sense allowed them to relax with each other again. With her declaration of the evening before, Amy had recovered from any feelings of intimidation and shyness that she might have had about the overall situation, and Harrison was all the more impressed and amused by her spirit and breathless turn-of-the-century reaction to his presence even though he was sad that their eight o'clock date had not materialized.

But to ease the situation further, as luck would have it, Amy had an antiques show to attend. So during the next few days, while she crated and packed some of her better pieces, Harrison began to work in earnest on some of the refinements for the house that he had envisioned. Out of necessity he found himself paying even more attention to Amy than he had already paid as he analyzed her needs and working habits in the house, which also afforded him some moments of pure risqué fantasy. At the same time, examining the construction of the house, he was increasingly amazed by

the many ingenious engineering concepts origi-
nally employed in it. Most were primitive and
often simple by modern standards but were nevertheless sound in their theory and advanced for
their time. The best example was the way in which
the house was designed to create natural air conditioning through the use of strategically placed ceiling fans, augmented by the opening of several
well-placed windows throughout the house and
vents in the attic, to take advantage of the prevailing winds from the ocean and the Chesapeake
Bay. It was while he was examining the vents that
Harrison came upon Amy in the attic.

She was sitting among some crates that she had
apparently been planning to take downstairs, but
for the moment her attention had been arrested
by the contents of an old trunk that sat open in
front of her. Strewn around the floor were all sorts
of items, including an old gadget that looked as if it
were filled with some sort of mechanized hooks,
and several stacks of books and paintings. She was
intently reading a large book near an open window in the sunlight. Tiny beads of perspiration
had dampened her face and hair, creating the
ringlets that gave her a wonderfully attractive
charm. Because of the temperature, her loose
blouse and shorts had evidently been adjusted to
uncover as much of her body as possible, and Harrison felt his mouth begin to water. Periodically
she paused while reading to look carefully at the
palm of her right hand.

"Amy?" he said.

She looked up, startled. "Yes," she answered. It was obvious that she was slightly embarrassed.

"I'm sorry to interrupt," he said with sensitivity. "I'm just trying to do something about making this place a little cooler."

She looked at him a bit strangely. "I don't understand," she said. "You must know central air conditioning in this house is completely impractical, and I'm certainly not going to ruin its appearance with those horrible-looking window units, not for just a couple of months of slight discomfort."

Noting her warm appearance, Harrison looked at her and smiled. "If you call this heat and humidity slight discomfort, I'd hate to think about what would be a major discomfort to you."

He looked nonchalant, but she could see he was stirred by some intense emotion, and she suddenly realized how she must look in her skimpy clothes. Amy was almost immediately on the defensive. "Well, of course, if you're not pleased with your accommodations, you can always—"

"No, for heaven's sake, that's the farthest thing in the world from my mind," he said with sudden exasperation.

Why, oh, why did everything always have to turn into an instant confrontation with her? Why was she making everything so hard? But then the challenge made the reward all the sweeter, he thought, and gave her a little grin. "Actually there's no need to even think of such modern things. My great-great-granddaddy has already taken care of it for you."

He walked around the attic, stooping here and there to make room for his tall frame, while Amy looked at him dubiously.

"What are you talking about?" she asked, her own academic interests slowly emerging.

"I analyzed the whole thing," he said as he walked to the far end of the attic, where he ran his hands over the wall until he found a small lever protruding next to an old vent. "First I entered the problem into the computer to see how I might solve it without compromising the aesthetics that are so important to you, and then I discovered that someone had already beaten me to it."

He groaned and pushed on the lever while Amy continued to look at him incredulously. There was a loud, rasping sound, and Amy felt the hint of a soothing breeze playing over her face. "There, you see," said Harrison. He walked over the floor, carefully examining it, and then shouted excitedly, "Aha!" He stooped and began to tug after he had wet a finger and followed the direction of the air current. There was another rasp, and then Harrison quickly went on to find several more wall and floor vents.

"You see, it's according to how the wind is blowing. You open and adjust various windows and vents that were built into the house." Harrison moved back toward the middle of the attic and looked up. He was almost beside himself with excitement as he pointed up. "Can you believe that?" he said. He looked around for something to climb on. After placing crates and other items indiscriminately into a pile, he climbed up for a better look.

Before Amy could caution him, though, his makeshift ladder gave way, and Harrison came tumbling down with a loud crash. Dropping her book, she ran toward him, sure that he had to be hurt. "Are you all right?" she asked as she automatically began to feel his arms and legs while brushing the dust away.

"I am now," he said with a lascivious grin.

Amy colored and immediately stopped touching him. "You could have really hurt yourself," she said sternly. "What on earth were you doing?"

He sat up with a grimace as he realized he had scraped an arm and bruised himself in several other places.

"You *are* hurt," said Amy, all concern again.

"No, I'm not," he said a bit sheepishly, "but if being hurt means getting this kind of attention, I'm not so sure I would mind."

"Cut it out," she ordered as suddenly she felt an easy camaraderie that was a great improvement over the nervous reactions she usually experienced with him in situations such as this. "So what's the big deal up there?"

"Another fan," he said incredulously. "An honest-to-God exhaust fan that will push out all the hot air from the house and suck in the cooler air from the water to air-condition the entire house naturally."

"That's impossible," said Amy, looking up. "It must have been put in by someone who owned the house before me."

"No," he said as he reached for her hands. "I'm telling you it's in the plans that you allowed me to study. It probably just needs to be fixed up a little. You yourself told me there were a lot of things in the house that were way before their time."

"Yes, that's true," said Amy, who was already feeling a vast difference in the temperature of the attic.

Harrison stood up and pulled her with him to the window near where she had been sitting. He reached up and found a lever to open yet another vent and quickly adjusted it to the flowing air currents already in evidence. "You see," he said. "It works. It's so simple it's almost ridiculous, but that's what makes it ingenious!"

As the air grew perceptibly cooler and Harrison found more floor vents, Amy suddenly looked at him dubiously. "Does this mean you've already opened the house downstairs?"

"Only where it was needed to take advantage of the prevailing winds today," he said.

"Oh, no," she said in real agony.

Harrison looked at her and was again completely mystified. Just when he was expecting some real gratitude and perhaps even a small word of praise, she was regarding him as if he were some sort of monster.

"The dust," she said in despair. "It'll ruin the furniture. I'll never be able to take care of the antiques if we do this."

She looked like a distraught little girl, and Harrison immediately understood her dilemma.

"There's no need to worry," he said with sincer-

93

ity. He went to her and pulled her into a friendly embrace as visions of all the sparkling clean and polished furniture in this house came instantly to mind. "I've already put together plans for a refined sonic device that will zap every particle of dust in the house. You won't even have to polish anything if it turns out the way it's supposed to."

Amy looked at him in disbelief. "You're crazy," she said, and stepped out of his arms. "You're talking about some wild fantasy or something which you are *going* to do. In the meantime, the house is filling up with dust! We have to close it up right away!"

She turned to leave, obviously intent on undoing all his work. He reached out and grabbed her before she could get away. "Now just a darned minute," he said, his voice rising perceptibly and showing a hint of sternness.

But she squirmed away and went clattering down the stairs while he looked after her ineffectually. To her surprise, as she moved down, she found that the interior of the house really was comfortable, and there was a wonderful scent of summer garden throughout the rooms. She looked around, expecting to see every window open, only to find that she was going to have to search for the offending apertures.

"This is incredible," she said aloud as she walked around in complete amazement, and all her admiration for Harrison I came flooding back to remind her what a truly wonderful man he must have been. She glanced up to see young Harrison watching her while he came down the steps, and she looked at him with eyes filled with sincere respect. "I'm sorry," she said as he came close. She looked around in obvious pleasure. "This is just absolutely wonderful. Actually, if we just remember to keep the unfinished rooms closed off, the dust should be pretty manageable."

"I told you I'd fix that, too," he said, feeling very pleased with himself.

"So you did," she answered. She gave him an indulgent smile. "But really it's not necessary. It's clear that the dust problem won't be as bad as I imagined. Besides, I enjoy polishing and cleaning."

Shaking his head, Harrison was already busy with better solutions to the problem. Completely uninhibited now, he reached out to clasp her in a friendly hug. "It will really be super, though," he said with continued enthusiasm as he led her back toward the stairs, "when we get that attic fan working."

"I think you're right," she said as they returned to the attic.

"Yes, let's take another look," he said. "And then I'll help you get those crates down."

"Thanks," she said. The interaction between them was growing increasingly easy and natural. "That would be a great help."

Using a real ladder this time, Harrison needed only a few moments to examine the fan before he returned to the safety of the attic floor. "No problem at all," he said, dusting his clothes where they had touched the high rafters in the roof. "Now tell me what you were up to that was so interesting when I came up."

She flushed and looked away, and for a second both of them thought the easy familiarity they were enjoying was going to be lost. Then Amy gave him a delightfully conspiratorial smile. "I just found another old trunk," she said. "It seems I always manage to find something new whenever I come up here."

Harrison glanced toward the piles she had carefully made and saw the book she had flung aside. "So what did you find?"

"Well, among other things, I think this is some kind of early knitting machine," she said, picking up the gadget he had noticed earlier. "It's obvious that these are needles something like crochet hooks that could be mechanized with this lever to—"

"And what is this?" said Harrison, who interrupted her with a mischievous glance when he remembered that she had been studiously studying her palm.

The cover of the book said *Madame Dussard's Book of Palmistry*.

Amy laughed and grabbed for it. "Never mind," she said as he quickly hid it behind his back, barely managing to keep it out of her reach. Giggling, she lunged after him and nearly toppled him over as she landed against his chest.

"Uh-uh-uh," he said teasingly. "Mind your manners now."

"You're the one who is being insufferable," she said, pushing herself away from him.

96

"No, now let's just take a good look at this," he said as he held the book up and tried to open it to the first page.

"Oh, go ahead," she said, realizing how silly this had become. "Actually it's rather interesting."

"I could tell," he said drolly.

"No," she said, trying to salvage some of her academic dignity. "It is an ancient art, you know, and this is obviously a testament to some of the social fads of the time. Something like yoga or aerobic exercise today."

"And obviously no one would have his or her palm read today," he said, tongue in cheek.

"Not as often or with the same degree of seriousness as people did then," she said firmly while her eyes began to flash with fiery impatience. She reached for the book. "You see, this obviously belonged to your great-great-grandmother Aribella. I think this trunk was filled with things that belonged to her, and she apparently painted all these pictures. I think she had real talent."

Harrison appeared interested and stooped to take a better look. "Amazing," he said, and his voice softened. "It's strange to sit here and look at things that may have been used or created by someone who is actually a part of me, yet I know absolutely nothing about her."

"Well," said Amy, who felt exonerated now, "this book should really be interesting to you then. Aribella seems to have been quite a charming eccentric."

"Are you sure she wasn't your relative instead of

97

mine?" His eyes were dancing as he reached out to give her a friendly pat.

"I'm not the one who is talking about sonic dusting machines and mind-activated computers," she said meaningfully.

"Touché," he answered with open admiration. "So what does the book say?"

"It tells you how to read the different lines in a palm and to some degree to read the future but, more important, how to assess the characteristics of the person being read."

"Oh?" he said as his carnal instincts leaped to attention. "Care to give me a demonstration?"

"No, it's all a bunch of hooey, I know that," she said, and gave him a little smile.

"So what does your palm say?" he insisted. "I saw you reading it."

"I was only curious," she said, her face growing a bit warm.

"So tell me," he said. "I'd like to know what's in store for you."

"Would you now?" she said. Her eyes met his in a full blaze of challenge, and a coy little smile began to play over her face. "I don't think that would be a wise move on my part, now would it?"

"So okay," he said agreeably. "Read mine."

"You can't just pick up a book and know how to do this," she said, thinking that the whole thing was suddenly going way past silly and ridiculous to some degree of nonsense that she couldn't even fathom.

"Sure you can," he said, reaching for her hand. "Let's see now. Lifeline."

"No, stop," she said, suddenly strident.

He looked at her in puzzlement. "What's wrong?" he said.

She wasn't kidding. A bit concerned now, he held her hand firmly and looked closely at the lines in her palm. "Hmm," he said after a moment of silence. A tiny grin appeared around his lips as he deliberately ran his hand over hers. "Can't tell a thing." He looked into her eyes. "Maybe you'd better read mine."

"Don't be silly," she said as she tried to pull her hand back. "It doesn't really make any sense."

But he held firm and slowly began to read from the book. "Lifeline. Sign of health, vitality, and outlook on life, all of which influence your lifespan . . ." He looked closer until he had identified the matching line in her palm, ignoring her continued protest. "Should be long, clearly marked, and unbroken—"

He looked up at her, clearly perplexed. "Yours is broken," he said. There was a note of alarm in his voice.

"I told you it was silly," she said, and pulled her hand away. "Look at your own and see what it says."

Clearly caught up in the mischief of the whole thing now, he stuck out his hand. "Tell me," he said. "After seeing yours, I don't know if I can stand to look at mine."

"No," she said, feeling more ridiculous by the moment.

"I insist," he said as they both began to feel the

magic that naturally started to accompany their touching each other.

Feeling silly but also somehow content, Amy traced the lines in the palm of his hand as she searched for identifying notes in the book. "Well, apparently," she said as she looked at his long lifeline, "you are forceful and would rather die than not have the last word."

"That's not true," he said, sounding a bit aggrieved as he moved closer to take a better look. Their faces were only inches apart, and the chemistry of the closeness began to take its effect. Harrison felt the hunger within him emerge as Amy too experienced the warm vibrations of their intimacy. "So I guess that means there's nothing to worry about so far as yours is concerned either." His laugh reached out to caress all her senses.

"I wouldn't be so sure," she said. "Seems to me that's not so far off target for you."

"Never," he said, his voice deepening to a new degree of intimacy. "I'm a perfectly easygoing guy who just does his own thing."

"Precisely," she said, recalling the number of changes he had already made in her existence in just a matter of days and the way he had ignored all her protests.

"So what does that say about you then?" he asked. He traced the broken line in her hand and reached up to give her a small nibbling kiss.

She giggled and tried to evade his intimacy. "Oh," she said flippantly, "it probably means I have two lifetimes to live."

"Makes sense," he said, and he reached up to

pull her closer, unable to restrain himself any longer. He opened his mouth for a deeper, far more encompassing encounter with her lips and tongue. Instantly deluged with warm, delicious feelings as she gave in to the sensation of his passionate, probing kiss, Amy felt her mind swirling in recognition of some deeper subconscious revelation while he continued to talk around his caresses. "That's why you're here in this house, living among the old and the new."

"Sounds too profound for me," she said, realizing she was very much enjoying the intimacy that they were sharing, an intimacy that had just seemed to evolve from nowhere and now seemed completely natural. Giving him a long look while he lazily examined her smoldering eyes, flushed skin, and swollen lips, she reached for the book again.

"Perhaps we should read a little farther," she said while she gave in freely to the pleasurable feelings that were beginning to overtake her entire body.

"I'd rather continue what we're doing," he whispered, reaching out to trace a ringlet of her hair on her forehead. "You know," he said, raising the palm of her hand to his lips and looking into her eyes, "I find you more than just attractive."

Amy waited in sweet expectation for him to go on.

Encouraged by her response, he reached into his heart and just said what he felt at that moment. "I want to be much more to you than just an acquaintance or Harrison the first's descendant." He reached out to give her another nibbling kiss and ran his fingers down her arm.

Amy felt as though a wonderful fabric were being woven about them. She could almost sense everything he was going to say and felt no need to respond, sure that he understood her acceptance of what he was saying. The bond, clearly mirrored in their eyes as they sat for a long breathless moment and searched each other's faces, brought them closer and closer until he tucked her hand into his. "Come here," he said softly. He pulled her into a one-arm embrace, and they sat side by side against the old trunk.

Harrison couldn't believe the tender intensity of his feelings. The moment he had dreamed of could very well be at hand. But somehow, instead of pursuing it in a more robust, physically satisfying way, he suddenly found that he simply wanted to be near her, close to her, just like this.

Amy was completely immersed in the moment, too, as she felt the rhythm of his heart through the pulse of his hand. In a natural way she found herself settling back in his embrace, enjoying in the cool breezes that blew over them. As if following some preordained path, they began to talk in the searching way of a couple who wants and needs to know everything about each other.

"So you've always been plagued with these wild thoughts," said Amy more than an hour later as she stretched and then settled against him again.

"I guess so," he said as he looked at her and saw in her everything that he had ever wanted in a woman.

She began to smile and picked up the book about palmistry. "Well, I wonder if we could find out why from this," she said teasingly.

"No. It doesn't matter where they come from. They're a part of me and always will be. I just have to respond to them," he said with a decided leer.

She laughed, and he pulled her across his lap into a demanding embrace. Making no move to resist, she welcomed his lips, which met hers in a wild, fiery collision. "I'm serious, Amy," he said, leaving a track of warm caresses on her face and down the inviting trail of her neck. "I think we could have something very special together."

"I may be inclined to agree," she said coquettishly, "but I'm beginning to feel like a naughty child who is doing unspeakably outrageous things in the attic."

"Hold that thought," he said, moving to stretch out next to her on the floor. " 'Naughty' is definitely the operative word here."

Giggling, she relished the feel of his hands and the warm sensuality of his kisses while they continued to pet and court in a wonderful innocence. But slowly their passion grew stronger, and they felt as if electricity were flowing through their bodies. Drawing closer and closer, Harrison knew she was increasingly receptive to his advances, and the hunger that had driven him almost from the moment he had first seen her depleted his patience as the fires of passion demanded their due. Moving to claim complete fulfillment, he began to pull her clothes away while his hand reached to cup her breast.

Moaning, Amy was nearly as wanton as he. The spark of her earlier feelings began to rage in a wild, overwhelming way. But as the setting summer sun began to spread its rays across the room, dust danced in its warm beams, and Amy knew she didn't want to have this moment here, in this place, in this way. "Wait, Harrison," she whispered. "Let's make this perfect."

"Seems perfect enough to me," he said, pulling her beneath him insistently.

"No," said Amy in a bit of a panic. She had nearly allowed this to go too far. Harrison was obviously out of control, manifested by the hardness of his manhood against her thigh, while her own body continued to respond, encouraging him. "No. Not here."

"Why not?" he demanded, looking fleetingly around.

"The floor is hard," she gasped. "Everything here is filthy. We're filthy!"

The bulletlike sounds of the words and the very words themselves reached Harrison, and his ardor began to recede. Looking around and then seeing the wild emotion in her eyes, Harrison thoroughly agreed. In spite of his deep, almost painful physical need, he knew that his ultimate moment of triumph and sharing with this magical woman could not take place in such surroundings. "I'm sorry," he said, and immediately released her. More than a little chagrined, he looked away and then began to smile as his adventurous spirit immediately came to the rescue. "Sure was fun though, wasn't it?"

Amy avoided his eyes.

Not wanting to lose the ground he had gained, Harrison reached out and tipped up her chin, forcing her to look at him. "Another time, another place," he said softly.

A small gasp escaped from her. She fleetingly recalled how many times she had had searing fantasies in the past. But then this was nothing like that. No, not at all. "Perhaps," she said with a shy smile.

Harrison gave her a long, calculating look. "No, not perhaps," he said, "but for sure when the time is exactly right."

An unspoken bond brought them together again as she nodded her head. Her eyes glistened with emotion. He helped her to her feet and looked fondly down at the trunk. "I think that I'll always remember this afternoon," he said. "I don't know when I've spent such a wonderful time in an attic."

She smiled in response, and her spirit soared, happily freed of all inhibitions, while he went about gathering up the crates she had selected earlier. "Show me the way," he said, starting for the steps. Rushing to help him as he juggled the awkward boxes, Amy brushed close to him while she held the door open. It was like pouring fuel on smoldering coals, and the flames of their passion leaped up in searing demand. Struggling to manage his load, Harrison looked at her with naked desire. "Just don't forget," he rasped as she met his eyes in mutual understanding, "when we're done here, we have some unfinished business to take care of."

CHAPTER SIX

An hour later, with nearly all the crates safely deposited in the parlor, a marvelous teasing camaraderie had emerged between Harrison and Amy tinged with expectancy and sensuality. And as the events of the afternoon replayed in Harrison's mind, he started to chuckle. Amy, removing packing cloths and paper from some of the wooden boxes they had brought down, gave him a perplexed look.

"You know," he said, his attention beginning to focus elsewhere, "there could be something to all this palm reading. They already have high-tech computers that screen people's palm prints in high-security areas—"

"Enough," said Amy with a saucy toss of her head. "Is there nothing sacred to those things? I told you palmistry is an art. The next thing I know you'll be trying to mass-produce the Mona Lisa." She looked derisively toward the John Needles desk where the computer was housed.

"Maybe so," he said, obviously enjoying himself. "And just think. If we used Madame Dussard's

107

book as a program, we might get rich telling fortunes!"

Realizing he was teasing her, Amy grinned and looked away. "That doesn't deserve an answer," she said. "Besides, computer horoscopes have been around for ages." She feigned a little yawn and gave him an appraising look. "I don't know about you, Harrison James the fifth, but I think I'll take a bath."

The moment seemed to stand still as he gave her a piercing look. "Need some help?" he asked with a teasing arch to his eyebrows.

His voice was deep and inviting, filled with sexual innuendo. In one instant all the passion, longing, and need they had shared in the attic came flooding back. Their eyes met, and Amy's lips parted slightly. "Perhaps," she said as she gave him an openly wanton look.

In a microsecond he was across the room and she was buried in a wild demanding embrace in his arms. Their tongues met and their kisses were savage as he picked her up and headed for the stairs.

In one magical instant, while they moved quickly up the stairs, Amy knew she had found the way to fulfill all her fantasies. Harrison's lips were hot with passion, ravishing her from her brow down to her breasts, as they neared the door to her bedroom. The huge four-poster bed stood like a welcoming beacon, and this time there was no controlling their passion or, for that matter, any desire to do so. Without pause Harrison headed for the bed but then turned toward the bath, already imagining the touch of her skin in the soapy water. In that moment every fantasy that he had ever experienced seemed to come to life. He reached for the faucets on the old squat tub as he deposited Amy in it. "Is this what you had in mind?" he asked, a devilish gleam in his eye.

"Not on your life," she whispered, reaching for the buttons on his shirt.

Delighted beyond words, Harrison quickly stripped away her skimpy summer clothes and turned on the water. Fragrant steam rose around them as the tub filled, augmented by the aromatic salts Amy quickly added. "There's room for both of us," she said invitingly while her eyes narrowed in seductive desire. Having pulled his clothes from his lean, muscular frame, Amy relished the feel of his hard body as they both sank into the deep recesses of the massive old bathtub that resembled in many ways the luxurious sunken Jacuzzis often found in expensive modern homes.

What I could do with this, thought Harrison fleetingly, but the thought was quickly flung away as he pulled her close and felt his own vibrant response to her body. In warm, expectant satisfaction Amy felt the strength of his manhood next to her. She opened her mouth to his kisses, aggressively seeking his tongue, as his hands moved over her, finding the softness of her breasts and titillating the tips of her nipples, while his legs reached out to clamp her close to the length of his body.

"Amy, Amy." He sighed as he gave in to the

sublime driving sensation of the experience. "I can't believe this is really happening."

"Nor I," she said. She reached out with a sponge to wash his shoulders, but she abandoned the gesture to run her hands over his chest. She delighted in the crispness of his tangled hair. Teasingly she traced the edge of his nipples, responding to his lead as he caressed every part of her body with sweeping hands and lips.

Their kisses grew deeper and deeper as their bodies demanded more and more. Pulling her close and probing with his manhood in a silken way, Harrison knew he could wait no longer. With a masterful motion he pulled them from the water.

Laughing in sexy appreciation, Amy grabbed a huge soft towel from the towel rack and flung it around them as they walked purposefully toward the bed. Adding yet another dimension to the titillation they were already experiencing, she began to towel him dry, rubbing the fabric over his body in a rough, exhilarating way as crystal drops of water shook over their faces from their dampened hair. Driven by the heat of their need, Harrison dropped with her to the bed and sank into the deep softness of the huge feather mattress. Almost mindless because of his driving need, he ravaged her with hot, demanding kisses, reveling in her unrestrained response as she matched his ardor.

"Now," she cried as she pulled him closer and opened her body in invitation. "Now."

Harrison pulled her beneath him and teased her with the tip of his manhood as she anticipated the moment she desired. Writhing to accommodate him, she met his eyes. He smiled and moved to tease her even more. With deliberate motions he brought his strength over her length, luxuriating in the delicious, silky feel of ever more heightened anticipation. He reached down to increase the pressure of his ardor, guiding his manhood skillfully to the spot of her most intense pleasure. Gasping, Amy pulled him ever closer, undulating faster and faster, as she begged him with her eyes and hands not to stop. Excited almost beyond endurance, he reached out to cup her breasts, which he then kissed and caressed. He suckled in intense pleasure until he could bear it no longer. With a supreme sigh of capitulation he released his restraining hand and slid deeply into her, melting into the strongest passion he had ever experienced. The hot recesses of her body welcomed him, meeting him thrust for thrust as his ardor increased even more and grew to proportions he had never imagined.

"I'm in heaven," he murmured as he opened his eyes and saw her wanton body beneath him. Inspired by the raw savagery in her eyes, he delved even farther, pushing himself to the limits of his physical prowess as he felt a gratification stronger than he had ever imagined overtaking him. Amy's hands reached for him. They traced the sinews and muscles of his arms and back while he reached for the limits of his power. She pulled him closer. He felt himself being persuaded into her embrace while the rest of him plunged to her very depths in delirious pleasure. In a frenzied moment of need, she held him and then turned in one swift movement. In a flash she was over him, riding him and the passion they shared. He found himself reaching for her breasts as they swayed invitingly toward his lips. In abandon they both gave in to the moment, unmindful of the sheen of perspiration that covered each of them. With deep emotion, as Harrison felt himself growing nearer to release, he pulled her close, knowing he wanted to nurture her and hold her beneath him when he had his ultimate moment of triumph. With a wild yell he captured her lips and clasped her in his embrace while they moved once again in unison to the position he desired. Overcome by his strength and mastery, Amy smiled in low-lidded, sensual satisfaction, glorying in his strong response to her challenge for supremacy.

"Love me," she whispered as she felt the urgency of his motions increasing. "Love me."

Holding his shoulders and reaching for the tangle of his hair, she felt her body arching in response to his as he thrust deeply and masterfully, until at last he shuddered to a final moment of impassioned need and then sank into sublime satisfaction. He felt the waves of her response coming up to clasp him and hold him lovingly captive while they both gasped for breath and looked into each other's eyes, happy with the moment and their mutual response.

Struggling to quiet their breathing and their racing hearts, they reached out to soothe and pet each other, content to stay in the grasp of their passion for yet a few moments more. Savoring the continued gentle aftermath of the wild vibrations that had just lovingly assaulted them, they searched each other's eyes and contented themselves with warm, sweet kisses. Tracing Amy's features with his lips, Harrison felt wonderful, sure that he could never want more from an intimate experience than this. In the same instant he knew he could never allow this moment to escape him. He had to have it again and again.

"I think I love you," he said softly to his own as well as to Amy's surprise. "I've never known anything like this."

Amy smiled, delighting in his words, happy that he felt the way she did. She had given him her supreme passion. She had been dreaming of this for more time than she cared to admit.

Then she felt a bit silly. A small, foolish smile began to play over her face. It was ridiculous to compare her sophomoric fantasies with the experience she had just shared with him. Harrison was everything a woman could ever want in a lover, she thought as she met his radiant eyes filled with tender passion. "Let me know when you're sure," she said with a loud, throaty lilt to her voice. She reached out to caress his face. "Tell me what I can do to make it final."

Impressed with the worldly sophistication of her response, he grinned in lascivious mischief. "Just go on doing what you're doing," he said as he felt her soft hands moving through the crisp down on his chest. "I don't know what more I could ever want."

"Hold that thought," she said as she rose on one elbow and traced his features with a finger.

Delighting in the titillation created by the edge of her tapered fingernail, he reached out to clasp her hand and held it to his lips. "I can't imagine life without you," he said as she smiled happily.

Captured by the moment, each searched the countenance of the other, looking for every nuance of emotion that might be there. It was only when Amy saw Harrison I's portrait out of the corner of her eye that she looked away. The directness of his stare, the almost accusatory stance that she suddenly perceived unnerved her, and she stiffened and abruptly pulled away.

Following her glance, Harrison looked at her strangely and then forced her gaze back to his own. "What is it?" he asked as he felt the tenseness in her body. "What's come over you?"

"Nothing," she said as she felt herself flushing. She forced herself to relax, remembering again the soft but insistent strength of his body and the way she had responded to it. "For a second there I guess I almost felt he was watching us."

"Well, he certainly had an eyeful," said Harrison, who turned to meet his great-great-grandfather eye to eye. The robust laughter that erupted from him did even more to unnerve Amy. Its very sound grated on her in an annoying way.

"Don't be uncouth," she said, suddenly assuming her shy turn-of-the-century exterior.

"I'm only teasing," said Harrison. His eyes came back to her, and he reached tenderly out to trace the moist ringlets of hair that surrounded her face.

"I know," she said hastily. "But I just don't want anything to sully the moments we just shared."

"Sully?" He laughed. He couldn't restrain the amusement that filled his voice. "Surely now, *Miss Amy*, this is not the first time you've had such an ethereal experience."

She flushed even deeper and looked away. Harrison suddenly found himself a bit breathless, too. While his response had been totally unthinking, all of a sudden her reply was of absolutely earthshaking importance to him. In a flash of insight, he knew that he never wanted to share this sweet ingenue with anyone, nor did he want anyone else to have ever experienced what the two of them had just had.

"And what if I haven't?" she asked a bit defensively, pulling a little farther away from him. "I know most women are supposed to be so worldly and experienced today, especially at my age, but I guess I've always wanted it to be especially right before I gave of myself completely."

"You mean, you were a virgin?" said Harrison, absolutely incredulous at the very thought.

"No, of course not," she said, capable of handling herself in a matter-of-fact way as she felt no need to restrain herself with him in any way. "I foolishly managed to sacrifice that when I was much younger in the wild pressures of my youth, but I soon learned that I wanted far more than those earlier experiences ever provided."

"So your heart is pure and completely unfettered," he said teasingly, reaching out to smooth her brow.

115

"Oh, cut it out," she said, and pushed his hand away. She laughed and reached down to kiss him. "Let's just say I've always wanted the very best of everything in the traditional sense of the word." She finished with a prim little look.

"Oh-ho-ho," he said, pulling her close. "I trust that I haven't disappointed you?"

"Well . . . maybe there could be a bit of improvement here and there." He found the impishness in her eyes tantalizing.

"Oh, really," he said with a decided leer. "Care to be more specific? Perhaps you'd like to give me a demonstration."

They both felt the instant response of his body, and Amy smiled, wantonly delighting in her power to arouse him so quickly and completely.

"Another time, another place," she said wickedly as she realized how truly content she was in this moment.

Laughing, he kissed her again. Still the victim of her teasing arousal, he pulled her close to him and relaxed. Her hair spread over his arm while he cradled her in a loose embrace. "I'll hold you to that," he said. "Just so long as I know I'm your one and only."

Again he was caught up in the meaning of an unthinking utterance as he realized that while he had declared himself to her in a serious way, he had yet to hear such a declaration from her. "I am your one and only, right?" He suddenly raised himself and looked into her eyes.

"That remains to be seen," she said coquettishly.

116

"I may have just discovered a whole new means of expression."

"You can tease all you want to, but I know that what we just shared was more than a passing experience."

Her eyes grew round with emotion, and her smile deepened. "I'm glad," she said, running a finger tenderly over his lips. "I'm truly glad you think that way."

For a long moment the room was silent as each tried to fathom the meaning of the other's emotions. "You know," said Amy, moving a little closer to him, "I think I've learned something very important today."

"You have?" he asked as he wondered now where her sometimes erratic thoughts were about to take them.

"Yes. I've learned that real life is far more satisfying than any fantasy could ever hope to be."

He seemed surprised.

Amy didn't know why she had said it, but somehow she felt compelled to go on. "I have a bit of a confession to make," she continued, watching his expression carefully. "I really must admit that I have been more than a little obsessed with Harrison the first over there, and somehow today it's as if everything I ever dreamed about has been fulfilled. I'm beginning to think you were meant to come to me here in this house. The whole thing is just too incredible for me not to believe that."

Harrison gave her a searching look. He didn't like this. He didn't know why, but he didn't like it one bit. "What do you mean?" he asked gruffly.

117

Surprised by his reaction, Amy immediately felt silly. "I don't know," she said, and pulled away from him. "It was just a feeling. I probably should never have mentioned it."

Harrison forced himself to squelch the outrageous feelings that were nearly suffocating in their intensity when he saw how she was reacting. "I'm sorry," he said, and reached out to her. "I think I've already committed myself to you to such a degree that I'm actually jealous at the very thought of sharing you with anyone, real or imagined. I never expected . . ." He searched for words. "I certainly never planned it this way."

"Oh, you didn't, did you?" said Amy, suddenly feeling amused. She watched him struggle with a moment of insecurity. He actually turned a bit red, and she had a wonderful feeling of satisfaction. "And just what was it that you had planned?" There was a pixie expression in her eyes when she looked at him.

"I couldn't possibly tell you," he said. This was the wench he had spied on that first day, the one he had had so many wonderful fantasies about.

"I wouldn't be too sure of that," she said. She reached out to trail her hands over his ribs, teasing and tickling him a little.

"Don't get in over your head," he said warningly. "You know I'm a man who demands total satisfaction."

"I know," she said. She began to laugh uproariously. "That has always been completely evident."

But as Harrison joined her in her merriment, he saw her eyes pass ever so fleetingly over the por-

118

trait on the wall, and he wondered, in spite of his best efforts to squelch the thought, just whom she was really referring to. Realizing how ridiculous his feelings were, he finally opted to enjoy the moment and was happy to give in to his urgent desire to pet and love Amy in continued sweet abandon.

"Will we have more moments like this?" he asked as they lay in the shadows of summer moonlight, completely content and comfortable with each other.

"I'm sure we will," Amy replied. She felt drowsiness beginning to overcome her. She could almost feel the spirit of everything that she had ever wanted coming to surround her. "I think I've been touched by the magic of your presence and the essence of your vitality."

Deeply moved by the poetry of her words, Harrison once again cradled her in his embrace. "I can't tell you how much that means to me," he said, and gave her a soft kiss. "I would never have believed such a thing could happen."

"Well, believe it now," she said with a tender smile. And for the first time in she didn't know how long, she went to sleep without her habitual dreams of Harrison I, content now to be held by the real man who lay sleeping beside her. When she awoke, her mind was filled with a precious sense of commitment that embodied everything anyone would ever want to give to a lover, partner, or friend. She was in love, and she never wanted her feelings to disappear.

Harrison was also caught up in the dream of

their existence as the next few days became one magical moment after another. But all too soon, when the problems of daily life began to intrude, moments of dissatisfaction appeared. It began with little things, mostly concerned with Amy's continued rapture over the past and the things it contained and with Harrison's continued obsession with the future. Somehow, in spite of the sweetness and tenderness that they shared, Harrison felt it even more important than before to persuade Amy to accept his way of looking at the world. But she, influenced all the more perhaps by the very depth and intensity of what she considered romantic old-fashioned feelings, clung tenaciously to her beliefs. She was, however, indulgent of Harrison's whims, laughingly encouraging him now as he worked on not only his brain wave computer development and programing but the laser–X-ray instrument as well. It wasn't that she was discouraging or in any way intolerant. It was simply that Harrison never had the feeling that she accepted anything that he was doing as truly worthwhile. He was almost infuriated by her unchanging attitude that the best had already been created and now must be preserved. In his most disturbed moments he actually wondered if that was how she had regarded him in her thoughts as well. After all, she had admitted her fascination with Harrison I. How was he, young Harrison, ever to know if she really cared about him or if she thought of him as a modern incarnation of his ancestor?

Fortunately, before Harrison became too upset,

Amy went off to the antiques show she had been preparing to attend. While she was gone, Harrison began in earnest to create the things which he was convinced would finally impress her, things that were not only useful but also worthy of true scholarly attention.

He began with the house. Her reaction to his discovery of the air-conditioning system and the shining respect and gratitude on her face spurred him on as he climbed and crawled about. He soon discovered that in addition to the sonic dusting, which he was already working on, he could easily implement throughout the house a series of mechanical arms which would function from one basic program in the computer. For fun he decided to create the system to be activated by palm prints. Amy's, of course, would have to be added when she returned. He wasn't doing anything which wasn't already commonplace in many modern factory assembly lines, but to challenge himself, he decided to include the as yet unsuccessful function of having the arms pick up and sort specified items according to a special code he was developing. Thus, when Amy returned, she would find that with a quick press of her palm to the hidden panel he installed in a kitchen cupboard and with another press of a specified code key not only would dirty clothes be put in the washer and dryer, but they would actually be gathered up, sorted, and washed according to specified instructions. The method was applicable to all the mundane tasks in the house: polishing furniture, cleaning, clearing of dishes and the placing of them in

121

the dishwasher right down to the ultimate pièce de résistance, a food preparation machine that went a step farther than the ice-cream machine because it selected and loaded ingredients after either scanning a recipe or getting instructions directly from brain waves. It was a magical process that would fit onto one disk that could easily be loaded in and out of the central computer as it had now evolved from its position in the John Needles desk.

Of course, he couldn't accomplish all this in the two weeks Amy would be gone, but he worked on it along with his official experimental project. Before he was finished, he also had a plan for rigging the lawn mower and other outside garden tools to operate automatically.

He smiled often, thinking of Amy going about her many tasks and how pleased she would surely be with these improvements of his. Almost as if pulled there by a magnetic force, he frequently gravitated to the attic when he found himself missing Amy more than he would have ever believed possible. They talked often on the phone, and his feelings grew even stronger when he studied the voluminous amounts of material she had left for him all about the house, material on his ancestors and parts of her dissertation.

Looking over some of the papers she had left him, he recalled the way she had presented them to him. "Well, you were interested, weren't you?" she had asked with a hint of primness when he looked at her questioningly. Her eyes were wide with expectancy and authority. "I mean, after all, that *was* supposedly the reason why you wanted to come here this summer."

Her innuendo was obvious, and a grin slowly spread over his face and into his eyes. "And Santa Claus eats reindeer meat for breakfast on Christmas morning," he replied.

"Don't be silly," she replied with a censuring look. "This really should be very interesting to you. I thought it would give you something to do."

"Oh, I'll have plenty of things to do," he said, glancing about the room and running his hand suggestively down her back.

"That's what I'm afraid of," she said with a little more forcefulness than she had intended. "Listen, I know you have some wild ideas floating around in your head, but don't get carried away."

His teasing mood immediately vanished as he suddenly felt a response that was somewhere between annoyance and paranoia. "What do you mean?" he asked tightly.

Noting his reaction, Amy immediately tried to set the situation right. "You know what I mean," she said. She reached up to give him a soft kiss while her eyes looked worriedly into his. "I think you know what this house means to me and the way that I want to complete it." Her sincere words just made Harrison feel even more jealous than before.

"Harrison," said Amy, really worried now, "what's wrong? Why are you acting this way?"

"I'm not acting any way," he said defensively. He was an intelligent, rational man. Why was he acting in such a childish way? But deep inside, he had to admit his annoyance with Harrison I had reached such proportions that he had almost grown sick of his name, let alone all these reminders of his ancestor's existence in this house. Yet there was also something about Harrison I that was fascinating. It was as if there were something yet to be learned, as if all the facts were not known. So it was a real quandary for young Harrison, but intuitively knowing he couldn't voice such irrational dissatisfactions to Amy, he managed to catch himself before he had gone too far. He mustered a smile and reached out to pull her close. "I'm sorry," he said, and swept his hands over her back and kissed her brow. "I guess I'm a little on edge about your leaving."

"You are?" she said. She pulled back and gave him a coy smile.

She was irresistible when she looked like that, and he realized he hadn't been too far from the mark. He just couldn't visualize life without her now. He wished only that he could be sure she had the same feelings about him. It was mind-boggling when he thought about it. He had truly had only one thing on his mind when Amy's sensual charms had first set his body on fire on that spring day when they had met. But now he found himself thinking of her as a precious jewel, too valuable to lose. How had that ever happened?

Amy was also baffled by her feelings. When she looked into Harrison's eyes, she saw the best of two worlds, and sometimes she wondered how she could be so lucky to have had her dreams and fantasies so wonderfully fulfilled. Yet there were still times when she felt terribly compromised. She was coming to recognize Harrison's genius, but his goals and philosophies were terribly distant from hers. Were it not for the supremely happy and fulfilling relationship they now had together as well as the sense of déjà vu she sometimes had, she wondered if there was really anything that they had in common. But when she saw that look of pain in his eyes a second ago, it had gone right through her. Not for one moment did she want to see such a reaction from him. It made her think that everything they were sharing was threatened and might easily be whisked away or shattered. "No, *I'm* sorry," she said, reaching up to smooth his hair and straighten his collar. "All I meant was that I'd like to know what you have in mind so I can understand it."

"Maybe I want to surprise you," he said. His eyes immediately lit up with happy anticipation.

"That's what I'm afraid of," she said, a little lump thudding into her stomach.

"No, no, I promise," he said, turning her toward the parlor. "You have to admit that you've been pleased with everything I've done so far, and I've really been watching you. The other day you spent nearly the whole day just watering plants and trimming hedges. Do you know what we could have done with a whole day?"

The naughtiness of his intimation, not to mention her own instant assessment, was too funny to resist. "Oh, all right," she said in mock capitulation. "But be sure you study these papers about the house before you do anything." She tossed her head, and a wry little smile appeared on her lips. "Besides, how much can you do in two weeks anyway?"

"Precisely," he said as he felt all his earlier excitement and enthusiasm returning. "But you don't have to go away on my account. I have absolutely nothing to hide."

"Just be sure it stays that way," she said. "I never was too big on outlandish innovations."

"So I noticed," he said dryly.

CHAPTER SEVEN

They had made love after that. Harrison caressed her, seeking out the silky places of erotic pleasure, and Amy reached up to meet his lips. Her arms were holding everything that was dear to her heart. Ecstatic because his caresses set her on fire, she maneuvered to massage him, a sign of her generosity and willingness to give him as much pleasure as he gave her. Harrison gasped when her hands traced his manhood, and he moved to return the pleasure she was creating. Her eyes were filled with passion as she urged him on with sweet, loving words.

"Don't stop." She sighed as she felt waves of pleasure coursing throughout her body. "I wish this could go on forever."

"It will," he said as his soft lips replaced his hands.

Moving in a circle the better to succor him Amy sighed in happy acknowledgment of the happiness and love they now shared. An insistent fury emerged, evidenced by the strength and hardness of Harrison's body when he suddenly pulled her close, coming back to suckle her breasts and kiss her lovingly. He slid into her and rejoiced in the wild reception of her body to his.

"Never, never, have I loved anyone like this," he gasped, "and I never want to love anyone but you."

Amy gloried in his words, happy beyond her wildest dreams as she joined him in the mad rhythm of their ecstasy. Together they reached a moment of high triumph and fulfillment and then spent hours caressing each other until at last they slept secure in the knowledge that they were meant to be together.

When Amy was gone, Harrison missed her desperately.

Feeling especially lonely one day, he went into the village and soon found himself fascinated by all the archaeological activity going on around him. By chance he happened to come upon a colleague of Amy's named Lawrence Hartman when he stopped to speak to Arthur, who was cleaning an old well that was obviously yielding some very interesting items.

"How's Miss Amy?" Arthur asked as he handed a waiting worker an item that was encrusted with green slime. It resembled some sort of teapot.

"You know Amy Kyles?" asked a man standing to the side, studiously puffing on his pipe.

"Yes, I do," Harrison replied, and began to size up the other man. "I'm—"

"Don't tell me," said the man as his eyes lit up with interest. "Let me guess. You're Harrison James, Amy's real-life reincarnation who has come to live with her."

Harrison couldn't believe the effect that these words had on him, and he took an almost instant dislike to the other man. "I don't know what you are referring to," said Harrison.

"Oh, don't take it personally," said the man. "We all love Amy despite or maybe because of her marvelous eccentricity. It makes her so . . . different. It only seems right that the ghost she has been obsessed with would somehow materialize."

Harrison smiled as he realized that the other man was harmless. "Good guess," he said, and offered his hand in greeting.

"It is extraordinary," said the man, accepting Harrison's hand. "By the way, I'm Lawrence Hartman."

They went on to have a lively conversation, while Arthur continued with his smelly drudgery, producing quite an array of junk in Harrison's estimation.

"What is all this about?" asked Harrison, strolling away with Lawrence.

"National historic site," said Lawrence. "Always sends everyone in a tailspin as people try to discover every piece of garbage that was ever thrown away in their backyards."

"You don't sound too respectful," said Harrison, laughing.

"Well, some of us are a little more reasonable than others," said Lawrence, "although I do find all this fairly interesting."

Harrison became aware of a touch of British accent as Lawrence continued to talk. Actually, once Harrison had discarded his initial reaction to

Lawrence, he realized that he liked the man very much. For that matter, Arthur was an interesting character, too, a welcome change. Earlier, when Harrison walked about, noticing all the Victorian houses in various stages of restoration, he had been suddenly struck by an almost overwhelming depression. It was as if everything here had stood still in time and as if all that was left were a constant caretaking task. The shops were quaint, and he remembered stepping into the Washington Inn in Princess Anne, a building that had been built in 1744. It was definitely interesting but decidedly old and creaky at the same time, Harrison thought. It did nothing to fire his imagination as it obviously did for everyone else. It just left him feeling old and without purpose. It was nothing like the exciting blend of old and new architecture that surrounded him at MIT in Cambridge. He thought of voicing some of this to Lawrence but decided instead to mention his laser–X-ray idea.

"But that's a marvelous idea!" exclaimed Lawrence after Harrison had outlined his proposal for the invention and how it could be used. "Do you really think you could get it together soon?"

"I don't see why not," said Harrison. "It's really fairly elementary."

"Oh, I'm sure it is," said Lawrence wryly, his admiration of Harrison evident. "I'd like to see it work."

"I'll see what I can do," Harrison replied, smiling.

After the two had parted, Harrison felt considerably better than he had earlier, but when he returned home, he still felt lonely and empty without Amy. Still, to his surprise he didn't feel any of the oppression that had plagued him in town. Somehow Amy's house didn't seem as old or depressing as the ones he had seen earlier. On the contrary, this house, in spite of its obvious historic authenticity, seemed new. He felt as if he had known the people who had designed it and lived here. For the first time he began to understand a little of Amy's obsession.

He went into the library and picked up the small picture of Harrison I. He carefully scanned his great-great-grandfather's face, seeking a deeper understanding of the man. Then he went back to the plans and papers Amy had left. After studying them for several minutes, he went rushing up to the attic. He hurried to the trunk Amy had opened on the day they had become lovers. After a moment's search he found the gadget that she had called a knitting machine. Could it be?

He examined it carefully and then went racing back down the stairs with the machine in his hand. He sat down at the big desk in the library and began to study the work of the man who was his namesake. For several minutes he tried to decipher some scratchy writing on the papers Amy had left, but it proved almost illegible. Nevertheless, Harrison was certain the gadget was important in some way. He recalled the pioneering work of a man named Charles Babbage in the early 1800s. He was actually the inventor of modern computer theory but had been disastrously handicapped by the limited technology of his time. His work had been inspired by a jacquard loom. Could Harrison I have been of the same mind?

Then Harrison V found a reference he couldn't understand. In faint lettering at the bottom of a page there was written something about a safebox in the hands of time. A shiver of excitement went through him as he tried to figure out its meaning. Suddenly, for the first time, Harrison James I became *very* interesting to Harrison James V. Young Harrison knew then he had a lot of personal investigating to do. He was about to get to know his family very well, and when he was finished, he was sure all of Amy's conceptions would be vastly altered much to his own advantage.

It was with purpose and enthusiasm that Harrison began to install various gadgets in the house. After a period of indecision he included the bathroom so he could manipulate the temperature control of the water with computers. In between, he spent every spare moment studying Harrison I's papers. After many long hours young Harrison slowly came to the conclusion that he was studying some primitive ideas for some very modern concepts. It was also clear that these were rough drafts of something that Harrison I had placed in a special place. That funny shiver went through him again. It was almost maddening in its intensity. He could hardly wait to talk to Amy about all this when she returned. Meanwhile, he worked earnestly on the laser-X ray, determined to use it for his own purposes now.

Amy came home filled with enthusiasm and high spirits. As she supervised the unloading of all her crates and directed their placement, Harrison couldn't believe how happy he was to see her again.

"Oh, I had such a good time," she said, rushing into his arms. "But I missed this place and you so much."

"In that order," he said a bit disgustedly.

"Why? Does it make that much difference?" she asked, giving his nose a playful tweak.

"Maybe," he answered, unable to resist her ebullience.

"Well, then I guess I'll have to do whatever I can to cheer you up," she said, a husky quality coming into her voice.

"Sounds good to me," he said. They both broke into happy laughter, and his lips captured hers. "My place or yours?"

"Make it ours," she said. "The Harrison James house of passion."

Harrison couldn't help feeling a little uneasy with her description of the house. "Skip the labels," he said engagingly. "Let's just get down to business."

"Will do," she said, and squirmed playfully away, "but first let me finish getting all these *priceless* antiques in."

They continued their playful banter while Amy completed the details of her unpacking. Later they sat and talked on the back porch, knowing the best part of their reunion was yet to come.

"So what have you been up to?" asked Amy in a lazy, relaxed way. She was dressed in a gauzy chemise that was low-cut and cool so that the evening breeze easily passed through its loose cotton fibers.

"I thought you'd never ask," he said as his eyes lit up. "Among other things I met your colleague Lawrence Hartman and saw Arthur."

He went on to explain his progress on the laser-X ray and the programming he was doing in the house.

"Are you sure you know what you're doing?" inquired Amy. She felt the beginning of a touch of tightness when she recalled how meticulous she had been in her restoration of the house. Somehow she could almost see Harrison I's eyes glaring at her in distaste. She squirmed uncomfortably, and Harrison grimaced as he noticed her movement.

"Of course I'm sure," he said. "In fact, it was almost as if this house were designed for just such developments. There are tunnels for vents and compartments for dumbwaiters and all sorts of little things that make my job easier. There was even an ingenious rope and pulley setup that I've just refined and adapted to electronic compatibility."

Amy gave him an uncertain look. "I'm not sure I understand what you mean."

"Well, it's simple," he said a bit impatiently. "I did just what you asked me to do and studied all the original plans for the house again. In the process I discovered some of great-great-granddaddy's other papers and ideas, and I'm beginning to suspect he was deeply influenced by the ideas of a man called Charles Babbage."

"What on earth are you talking about?" demanded Amy.

"I mean, I think some of his papers indicate that he was an ingenious inventor, probably way ahead of his time and possibly even involved in some pioneer computer theory."

"Oh, don't be ridiculous!" Amy snapped, her eyes suddenly filled with fire. She wasn't about to have all her fantasies and suppositions tampered with in this manner. She couldn't believe how very protective she was of her own conception of Harrison I until that very moment. The stridency of her voice shocked her as much as it did Harrison. "I mean," she said, trying to recoup some of her composure, "it's always been perfectly clear that Harrison the first was a sea captain. He writes constantly of his travels, and there are charts and all kinds of complicated things to support that theory."

"Do you mean those old papers filled with scratchy numbers and equations?" He gave her a piercing look.

"Yes, they're obviously navigation charts of some kind. Look at his picture. The uniform—"

"But you never checked to be sure?" asked Harrison unbelievingly. "A woman with your credentials and academic interests? For something as important as your doctoral dissertation?"

Amy flushed deeply, resenting the implications of his words. "That isn't something that would in any way be involved with the substance of my studies," she said, raising her chin haughtily.

Fascinated but at the same time annoyed by her

135

response, Harrison felt as though he had to press on. Intuitively he knew that something about this was crucial to his continuing relationship with her. "But weren't you even a little interested?" he asked. "For pete's sake, the other day you spent hours studying that book about palmistry. Certainly this should have been just as interesting. You said yourself this house was filled with things that were obviously early versions of objects we take for granted today."

"Harrison the first was probably wealthy enough to have employed someone who knew about all the latest scientific inventions."

This was now escalating into a full-fledged disagreement as both Harrison and Amy felt their tempers rising. "I'm telling you," he said, trying to control the fury in his voice, "the man designed this house and everything in it. He was into things that must have boggled the minds of everyone around him. He was a genius, no question about it!"

"And it obviously runs in the family," said Amy savagely as she took in the wild intensity of his look. She looked at him and smiled. For some reason, she felt incredibly gay and light-headed.

Harrison was immediately aware of the change in her mood and felt his own tenseness dissolve, too. "What are we arguing about?" he asked as he reached for her hand. "The only thing that matters is that you know me, Harrison James the fifth, and believe in what *I* am doing."

Amy's eyes softened, and the moonlight framed her face sweetly. "I'm sorry," she said as she responded to the touch of his hand. "Why don't we talk about this later?" He gave her a long, searching look, pleased that the tension was relieved, but somehow he was still filled with a small, uncomfortable sense of dissatisfaction. Amy realized it and immediately took steps to set it right. "So show me some of these great inventions of yours."

His reaction was immediate and enthusiastic. He grabbed her hand tighter and pulled her to her feet. "All right," he said, beaming. "I have only one or two that are really ready to go. The rest are in progress, and to complete the software, I have to register your palm print."

The look on her face was more than worth all his frenetic efforts while she had been gone.

"My palm print," she said as all her uncertainties came flooding back.

"Yes," he said proudly. "I just couldn't resist throwing that in."

"I can't believe it."

"Sure you can," he said, and pulled her toward the kitchen. "Remember the ice-cream freezer?"

She looked at him quizzically. "Yes, but surely you aren't thinking of filling the kitchen with contraptions like that for every little chore."

"One contraption," he said. He inhaled, and his chest expanded in pride and expectation. "One very miraculous contraption."

Amy felt as if she were watching a child in a toy store, rather than a grown man.

"Right over here," he said, ignoring her reaction. "Now I've expanded this idea so that I press my palm to the command center." He opened a cupboard door, and Amy saw a small panel installed there. "I then look into the little flashing light and think what I want to prepare. The program analyzes the electrical patterns of my brain, compares them until it finds an appropriate sequence in its memory, and then activates. For example . . ." He looked into the light. "Cinnamon rolls."

To Amy's amazement she began to hear tiny rumblings and clicks and a small aperture opened in the wall. Then a grotesque-looking machine that resembled something between a mixer and a robot emerged on a platform. "Now watch," said Harrison, savoring the look on her face. "I've added something that has never been done with anything like this. It's going to collect the ingredients as I say them, or I could just have it scan a recipe the same as the ice-cream maker, and then it will gather the ingredients from the proper shelves and do the whole thing, even put the rolls into the oven."

"You've got to be kidding," said Amy, who sat down weakly to watch. As a long metal arm unfolded and began to maneuver around the kitchen, she was nearly overwhelmed by a terrible sense of intrusion. She felt as if her warm, cozy kitchen had just become a cold metallic garage or factory of some kind. "I hate it," she said before she realized what she was saying.

Harrison gave her a stricken look while the machine went on about its business with an efficiency that was almost like a dream to him. "You hate it," he said in disbelief. He walked around and stood in front of her. "Do you know what technology like this could mean to someone who was handicapped? Why do you think I have a grant for this type of research in the first place? Do you know what this could mean to airplane pilots or the space program?" His voice took on the tones of a zealot. "Why, we're even trying to emulate the knowledge and thinking processes of different experts and geniuses. Future historians won't have to speculate about the great minds from the past the way you do. They might have access to them in a kind of space age immortality and continue to interact with them for ages. Actually the two of us are not as far apart in our thinking as you may believe."

Amy colored and looked away, ashamed of her outburst. "I'm sorry," she said, realizing how she must have hurt him. "It's just that I need to get used to this sort of thing."

Seeing her reaction, Harrison immediately relented. "No, I'm sorry," he said, his voice softening. "Sometimes I forget how far-out some of this must seem not just to you but to anyone else who is not involved in this field of study. But can't you see? I'm talking about not only mind-directed programs but software that would allow brilliant diagnosticians to reach hundreds more patients than they can today, great teachers interacting with thousands of students at a time. Sometimes it's almost as if today is history because we're actually blocking out modes of living that are decades away."

"I know," she said weakly, a hint of tears behind

her eyes. She couldn't believe how bad she felt about this. "That's what scares me sometimes when I think about you and me."

She stopped as an aroma of cinnamon filled the room and the timer on a microwave beeped. "What's that?" she asked.

"Just something of mine that I added," he said a bit nervously. "I would have starved while you were gone without a microwave in the kitchen."

She couldn't resist the look on his face as a smile escaped her. "All right," she said, and reached out to comfort him. "Does that thing get the butter for the rolls, too?"

"It could," he said in obvious relief. "But just this once I'll get it myself."

He touched the panel with his palm and then looked into the light again. As Amy watched, the machine tidied itself up and disappeared. Harrison had retrieved the rolls and served them grandly with a dish of butter. "*Voilà,*" he said as he sat down next to her and prepared to enjoy.

Amy took a big bite and gasped.

"Ughhh," she said as she nearly gagged and pushed her plate away.

"What?" shouted Harrison, looking at her unbelievably.

"It's awful," she said. "I'm sorry." Tears were starting down her face.

Harrison quickly took a large bite of the steaming rolls, which looked like perfect pastry specimens. He nearly gagged, too, as a revoltingly bitter taste filled his mouth. "Good Lord," he said, looking as if the world were coming to an end, "I don't know what could have happened."

"It doesn't know the difference between flour and baking soda," said Amy with immediate understanding. "Or salt and sugar."

Chagrin washed over Harrison as he looked into her eyes. "Computers can't taste," he said a bit inanely.

"Obviously," said Amy, and then giggled.

"I mean, I programmed it for textures and . . ." He looked around a bit wildly for a few seconds. "You know the computer is only as good as the programming created for it. That's where the whole thing is, and this just needs some refining."

"I'll agree with that," said Amy before she gave in to her mirth and began to laugh uproariously.

Realizing the problem really wasn't all that serious, Harrison easily joined in her laughter. "What's life without a little failure now and then?" he asked as he pulled her close. "But wasn't it something, Amy? Wasn't it something to see it work?"

"I guess so," she said as she wiped a tear away and continued to laugh.

"And the beauty of it is," he said, looking at her excitedly, "that all the basic software that I've created is adaptable to the entire house."

Valiantly trying to suppress her inner emotions, Amy watched as he showed her the other mechanical arms and devices that he was in process of installing.

"No more dusting, no more laundry," he said. "Why, when I'm done—"

"You'll have ruined my house," she said flatly.

"No, no," he said as he grabbed her arms and willed her to understand. "You've got to quit looking at it that way."

"But I'm not helpless," she said, and pulled away. "I don't need these things. I enjoy living here the way—"

"Harrison the first," Harrison V stated flatly. He was suddenly more impatient with this fanaticism than he would ever have admitted to in the past. "You prefer to look back and be locked in a time when—"

"We're arguing again," said Amy in a low voice. She raised her eyes and met his. "This isn't good," she said as she turned away. "We can't go on like this."

Harrison couldn't believe the panic that invaded him when he heard her words; nevertheless, he felt a sense of outrage, too. "You may be right," he said. "Look," he added as he grasped her shoulders awkwardly, "I'm only trying to help and at the same time do some of my own work. You can't deny that it's for a good cause."

"Well, then why aren't you doing it in your lab?" she asked while her eyes filled with tears. "Why are you coming here and ruining my house?"

"I'm not ruining your house," he said, responding to her emotion with a tenderness that was almost as puzzling as everything else that was happening to him. "Besides, don't you think I have a stake in this, too? I'm discovering things here with you this summer that I might never have known. Getting to know about my family is opening up all

142

kinds of things for me. For the first time I'm beginning to understand why I'm the way I am."

"Well, I wish I could understand it," she said, a little smile beginning to appear through her tears.

"I think you could if you'd really look," he said firmly. "Those papers of Harrison the first's that I was studying—"

"Let's not go into that again," she said a bit hastily as she felt herself beginning to retreat again.

"All right," he said. "For now."

He willed her to look at him and finally felt some sense of satisfaction when he saw affection in her eyes. "Look," he said softly as he pulled her into his embrace again, "I'm willing to go halfway with you. I'll make a real effort to become involved with some of the things you're doing if you'll do the same for me."

She smiled and pursed her mouth in agreement, for she realized how much he had come to mean to her. Just the power he had to manipulate her emotions right now was enough to make her understand that. "That's a deal," she said, and reached up to kiss him. "You can begin by helping me to get ready for an open house I've agreed to have in conjunction with the Old Princess Anne Days to help support the Teackle Mansion restoration."

He gave her a surprised look. "Boy," he said as he gave her another quick kiss, "remind me to check you out before I make any of these rash declarations again. This sounds like a lot of work."

"Well, maybe," she said with a smile. "Of course,

it means showing off my antiques, too. And just so you can really see what good you're doing, you can go with me to a wedding that's taking place at the Teackle Mansion next week."

"Sounds wonderful," he said unenthusiastically. She gave him a playful warning look. "I'd better get cracking with these gadgets so they can do most of the work," he added teasingly.

"Just help me with the yards and outside work," she said as she gave his chin a nudge. "I'll take care of everything else."

"That's easy," he told her. "The lawn mower has been ready to go since yesterday."

Amy stopped. "What does that mean?" she asked.

"Never mind," he said a bit smugly. "You'll see."

CHAPTER EIGHT

The mystery didn't last long, for Amy awoke the next morning to a thunderous, raucous noise. She reached over for Harrison and found the bed next to her empty. The scent of new-mown grass was coming in through the window as she groggily rose and stumbled toward it. "Harrison?" she called when she saw the lawn mower moving through the yard all by itself. She couldn't help the panic that ran through her as she thought of the priceless old plants and hedges that she had lovingly nurtured back to life and the painstaking care she had taken to maintain the formal atmosphere of the gardens that surrounded the house.

"Harrison? Where are you?" she called as she came down the steps and saw the computer sitting out, obviously in full operation on the open John Needles desk. "Oh, my God," she said, knowing her worst fears were about to be realized.

Hurrying out to the porch, she came upon Harrison, electrodes firmly in place on his head, assembling the other yard implements in some sort of color code only he understood.

"What are you doing?" she shouted over the

noise. She couldn't hide her expression as the lawn mower came up to the steps and then pivoted away before retreating to clear another swath. There was a new small box on its controls that caught her attention because of the blinking light.

"The yard work, what else?" he shouted. He looked away, and she could see that he was concentrating on another small flashing light as a mechanical arm came sliding out from a small side door of the house. It was self-contained on some sort of cart that resembled a small square wagon.

Amy quickly surmised that this was just another adaptation of the gadget she had seen in the kitchen the night before as Harrison looked at first the hedge clippers, coded in blue, and then the weed eater, in yellow. Quickly following his command with a short series of clicks accompanied by sounds of rolling wheels, two arms unfolded, picked up the designated tools, and traveled to obviously programmed destinations.

Trying not to think of the screwup that had occurred in the kitchen the night before, Amy flinched at the thought of what could be ruined here as she met Harrison's smiling eyes and swallowed hard. "Are you sure you know what you're doing?" she asked hesitantly.

She had begun to wring her hands, and Harrison winced. "I think so," he said dryly as his smile faded. "This is all pretty cut-and-dried." Not even her appearance in skimpily cut nightclothes could remove the bitter disappointment that he felt at her words.

"Well, I hope so," she said, looking toward the

fishpond, where the weed eater was busily working along the edge. But as thoughts of the upcoming open house infringed, she was far too busy with her own concerns to notice the look on Harrison's face.

Watching her with growing annoyance, Harrison found himself staring after her with increased agitation as she moved carefully toward the working machines. Looking at her, he forgot for a second that the whole operation was under his mental command, and his concentration turned elsewhere. And in just that much of an instant the situation suddenly deteriorated.

Amy was stooping over a flower bed when suddenly the hedge clippers went out of control. Before she could blink, they had taken a wide swath out of her carefully manicured boxwood hedge. The lawn mower was running erratically over the yard, mowing down everything in its path. "Harrison!" she screamed as she watched a section of a very old lilac bush come tumbling down. Afraid now for her own safety, she went running for the porch as the lawn mower came toward her. Thus far the weed eater had kept its damage to a minimum because it had unceremoniously plunged into the fishpond, but now, as Amy saw the water in waves and the destroyed lily pads, she could only hope that the fish had escaped unscathed. She was also more furious than she had ever been in her life. She ran toward the pond, unmindful of the continued crazy swaths of the mower and clippers, and reached for the handle of the weed eater.

"No, my God, don't touch that!" shouted Harrison, who tackled her. They went tumbling to the ground in a jarring fall. "You could be electrocuted," he gasped.

"Then shut it off!" she shouted back as she grabbed wildly for the electrodes on his head.

"I can't until I get into the main station," he yelled, pulling her out of the mower's path. They rolled in a wild tangle of bodies and legs while Amy tried to push him away, angry with him and trying to ignore her immediate physical response to his touch.

"Well, do it," she said, shoving him away. She got up and went racing after the lawn mower. She was growing sicker by the moment as the work of years was being ruined. Seeing that she was capable of protecting herself now, Harrison rushed for the main computer and hit the off switch. Everything came to a whining halt while an eerie silence slowly descended. "Deliver me," said Amy, looking around with the vacant stare of a victim in a war zone after a horrendous battle. "Dear God, deliver me."

Harrison was equally shocked when he surveyed the damage. He searched for better words but could manage only a trite and totally inadequate "Oh, Amy, I'm so sorry" as he stumbled toward her.

He paused and closed his eyes before he tried again. "The software was perfect when I—" A sigh of exasperation escaped him as his fists clenched, and he looked away. There was a crack in his voice when he continued. "It should have been synchronized to the brain waves—" He stopped in mid-sentence, realizing what had happened.

Amy just stared at him, her face deathly pale as she struggled for words. "Now what am I going to do?" she asked dully, and dropped a broken flower. The gesture and her air of complete defeat pierced Harrison. He had never felt so bad in his whole life. "The open house is just a few weeks away," she said. "I'll never be able to repair all this damage."

"Yes, you can," he said. "I'll help you and—"

"Oh, no, you won't," she snarled as her anger finally surfaced. "I think you've done about all that you're ever going to do around here."

Fully acknowledging her right to such feelings, Harrison made no effort to dispute her. Instead, he walked to the mower and began to move it away from the sundial, which it had shaved and scraped, leaving an ugly gash in the cement.

"No, leave it alone," said Amy, who came flying after him. "I don't want you touching anything!" Her eyes were flashing fire, and she was obviously out of control.

"I'm only trying to help," he said gently.

But as the sundial came into full focus, Amy felt her anger growing to even greater heights. The quaint old timekeeping device had been one of her favorite things. In fact, it was one of the reasons why she had decided to buy the house when it was little more than a ramshackle shell. Somehow, in spite of all of time's abuse, it had continued to stand in stoic stateliness, and now in just a few short minutes Harrison's genius had managed to do what time and lack of attention had not. "I don't want anything from you," she said in a low, ragged voice. "Can't you see that you've already done enough?"

Harrison was deeply struck by her anger, but he had invested himself in this relationship, and he wouldn't give up over this. "Amy," he said, stooping in front of the sundial, "I understand how you feel, and I don't begrudge you any of it. I know, saying, 'I'm sorry,' isn't good enough, but I promise you everything will be replaced or repaired in time for the open house."

"Oh, shut up," she said as she felt tears coming. "I can't stand any more of this." She went stumbling toward the house.

Harrison started after her, but as he rose, the cloth of his old jeans snagged on something and tore. He looked down and saw a sharp corner protruding from the center of the sundial base. "Amy," he called after her.

Struck by the excitement in his voice, she turned around. "Now what?" she asked, looking at him resentfully.

"Come here," he said.

Unable to avoid her own curiosity when she saw him examining the cement, she walked back hesitantly. "What is it?" she demanded when she saw the point of old metal.

"I don't know"—he paused—"but I think this just may be . . ." His eyes widened in sudden recognition. "Of course!" he said as he remembered the words "a safebox in the hands of time." "It's a

150

time capsule! Harrison the first put his ideas into a time capsule . . ."

"Time capsule!" she said incredulously. "Don't be ridiculous. And don't think you can divert my attention from what you've done." She stooped to take a better look and gave a final sigh of exasperation. "On the contrary," she said as she met his eyes forcefully, "I think you've damaged the plaque which has always fitted into the base perfectly. The words on it were worn away, but it was beautiful."

"No," he said, reaching for her hand. "I think you're mistaken. This is three-dimensional. Can't you see that?"

"No, I can't," she said. She gave him another deadly look and began to leave.

"Amy, please," he said, pulling her back down. She tumbled against him, and their eyes connected in one charged electric moment. "Don't let this come between us."

He held his breath, overcome with desire for her. Despite herself, Amy could not deny the physical response that threatened to carry her away. She felt her body warming to his in that now-familiar way and she was caught in the throes of indecision as she tried to make some sense of her feelings.

"Please," he said, holding her a little closer. "We've got so much going for us." His lips brushed over her brow.

She tried not to look at him as he waited for her to say something.

The silence lengthened, but he knew she was very angry.

"I'll do whatever you want," he said, softly nuzzling her face. "I'll do anything to make it right."

"Anything?" she asked, trying to come up with an appropriate retribution. Her eyes shone as they met his.

Realizing the extent of his capitulation, Harrison squirmed a bit uneasily. "Well, almost anything," he said.

"Anything is better," she insisted.

"No, this is better," he said as he pulled her close. He pressed his lips to hers for one long, agonizing moment. "This feeling is what we have to protect," he said when the kiss was over.

"I'm not so sure about that," she said, thrilling to his touch despite all her efforts to remain impassive.

"I'll make you sure," he murmured as his hands touched her breasts, setting her body on fire.

They gave in to a sweet, tender passion then as they continued to embrace. Shattered petals of roses became entangled in their hair. "I love you so much," said Harrison when he pulled her to her feet a few moments later.

She looked around and was suddenly awash with doubt again, surveying the damage to her gardens. "Right now that's a little hard to believe," she said wistfully.

"Believe it," said Harrison, suddenly vehement in his demand that she understand. "I promise you," he continued as he turned her around and forced her to look him squarely in the eyes, "I'll take care of all this. Everything will grow back and be the same as it was."

He removed a petal from her hair.

"But *that* rose is gone," she said mournfully as the petal fell to the ground.

"And another one, even more beautiful, will grow in its place," he said firmly.

With that he sent her off with a gentle pat to get dressed while he began to clean up the mess. But with those words it was almost as though the unresolved differences in their philosophies had been crystallized into a final form.

True to his word, Harrison painstakingly took care of the gardens, employing a landscape architect to work with Amy and restore as much as possible before the open house. Nevertheless, the backyard was conspicuously ragged-looking with several open swaths and other evident damage, so Amy sadly decided not to include that area in the tour.

The sundial continued to be a grim reminder of the damage as it had now become an object of curiosity to Lawrence Hartman and others involved with the historical site excavations. As it turned out, Harrison's guess about the time capsule excited a number of people once word got out.

"And you can bet Harrison the first was capable of such an idea," Harrison V was saying as he and Amy entertained Lawrence several days later.

Amy looked at Harrison V sharply and then turned back to Lawrence. "Well, I'm not going to

153

damage the sundial further," she insisted. "It seems like a rather preposterous idea to me."

"It certainly would be interesting to find out, though," said Lawrence, watching the two of them carefully. "Seems to me as if this is the perfect place to use that laser–X-ray invention you mentioned, Harrison."

"I can see you're ganging up on me," said Amy cautiously. "But this is going to have to wait until the open house is over. We've got too many other things to do first."

Lawrence and Harrison shrugged in convivial acquiescence. "I guess that settles that," said Harrison as they went in to have dinner.

"At least until you get the laser done," said Lawrence with a wink.

"Don't encourage him," said Amy with a touch of impatience. "He's about to drive me crazy with some of his insanity. He's even had the nerve to suggest turning the sundial into an atomic clock!" There was a decided touch of agitation to her movements as she served the salad.

"I don't think she's over what happened to the garden yet," he whispered, returning Lawrence's wink.

"And I may never be," she said warningly as a strained smile lit her face.

Thus, in spite of the reconciliation between Harrison and Amy, the incident in the yard had left a deep impression. There was still an obvious emotional estrangement between them. Now, while Amy prepared in earnest for the open house, she found herself growing more and more impatient as Harrison continued to work doggedly on his brain wave experiments and the laser–X-ray contraption. She found it necessary time and time again to give herself a stern talk when she discovered him stalking around the house with what looked to her like little more than a glorified metal detector. The fact that he also often had small black electrodes plastered to his head as he attempted to reach out to the computers in his lab at MIT just added to her consternation. She found it unbelievably maddening when he moved about completely engrossed, sometimes responding to a jerky rhythm, and she didn't know whether he was really working or just listening to records.

So, in spite of her best efforts, Amy found herself fighting a continuing sense of dissatisfaction and intrusion as soft bells and voices appeared all over the house. Harrison, in a particularly obtuse frame of mind, failed to comprehend how upset she was. It was almost as if he were now bent on coercing Amy into acknowledging and accepting his genius on his own terms. Slowly he attached almost everything in the house to the computer in the John Needles desk and created exceedingly sophisticated programming. Everything from coffee maker to clocks to the bath wat r temperature was included, and to make it even more unnerving, Amy never could figure out how he was manipulating these things.

In retaliation, while she continued with preparations for the open house, she began to slide more and more into the sanctuary of the past as she had always imagined it. Once again she found herself yearning for the peace and romanticism of the Victorian period. She began to use a very early model of a Singer sewing machine to fix a few of the curtains. And the easily understood mechanics of an old loom she had procured during her recent trip was far more to her liking than the intricate mind-boggling things Harrison was constantly fooling with. So while she prepared food in the old cast-iron pots, Harrison touched panels, wore electrodes, and looked into flashing lights. One thing, though, had not been completed because Harrison was reluctant to ask Amy to register her palm print on it. That was the mechanical arm to be utilized within the house.

In spite of all the problems they were having in their personal relationship, the world seemed somehow perfect when they came together in the depths of the feather bed each night. The four-poster, sitting in the middle of the room, was almost like a guardian angel protecting their love for each other.

Attending the wedding at the Teackle Mansion in Princess Anne was also a part of the truce. As it happened, the couple getting married had decided to create romantic antebellum atmosphere in keeping with the decor of the restored mansion. Not only did the bridal party wear clothing from the period, but the wonderful old house was bathed in candlelight and the garden was aglow with torches as guests arrived in antique carriages pulled by beautiful horses.

"Isn't it absolutely wonderful!" exclaimed Amy as she held on to Harrison's arm. Her face was aglow, and Harrison had never seen her look so beautiful in an exquisite crochet and open lacework dress covered with sequins and pearls.

"Yes, I have to agree that it is," he said, walking around the center parlor. "But I think it would be even more grand if small, subdued lights were in the garden. They could be operated by—"

"Oh, Harrison, don't start with that," she said impatiently. "Can't you just feel the history here? Just think, Thomas Jefferson and Madison and Monroe were once frequent visitors here."

He smiled indulgently and gave her hand a squeeze. They watched the intimate wedding ceremony in an almost breathless silence as first the house was filled with wonderful classical music and then the vows were exchanged with dewy sincerity as the couple looked into each other's eyes.

For the first time, while Amy and Harrison witnessed this sacred ritual, each of them began to have feelings that neither had really seriously considered before. It was as though until this moment they had just been gliding from one day to another, grateful for the experience of their sweet intimacy but wary of considering anything permanent. Suddenly, when they stood there in the hushed silence in the old, old house, witnessing the traditional oaths and promises that truly bound a man and a woman together, their hands came together in a supreme moment of real union. Amy looked at Harrison and saw her own emotion reflected in his eyes, and he gave her a tiny kiss.

"I love you," he mouthed.

She nodded in agreement and mouthed the same words to him just as the music came up again and the bride and groom, now man and wife, turned to greet their guests.

The reception, which was held in the same room and in the garden, was just as lovely as the ceremony, and when Amy and Harrison finally returned home, they fell into each other's arms and made sweet, tender love unlike anything they had ever experienced before. Holding her close, Harrison cherished every inch of her body. He reached out to share his feelings with Amy in a hazy communion as their eyes glazed and their tongues met in a fiery clash. Slowly nibbling and stroking, they aroused every tiny fiber and nerve in their bodies until at last they came together in a gentle, delicate rhythm. As his lips followed the trail of her neck and teasingly found the tips of her nipples until at last the warmth of her soft breast filled his mouth, his hands explored her most secret places. Gasping with pleasure, Amy gave in to rolling waves of pleasure while the room grew brighter and the aroma of roses filled her senses. Drowning in happiness, Amy reached out to stroke and caress him until at last the urgency of their growing need took over. Delving deeply as the rhythm of the moment drove him, Harrison looked into her eyes and gloried in the smoldering intensity of her desire. They loved each other with a tender passion until at last they lay next to each other, sweetly sated and happy beyond words.

"Promise me we'll always be together like this."

Amy sighed as snatches of long-ago dreams began to intrude.

"Always," he said, cradling her tenderly and smoothing back the locks of her hair. "Always."

Amy met his eyes and reveled in the happiness that washed over her. As their fingertips touched slightly but meaningfully, Harrison kissed her in a soft, feathery way. In that poignant moment it was almost as if he were seeing Amy for the very first time in an all-new light, and he cherished everything that she had come to mean to him.

After that, as they settled into a peaceful sleep, seemingly all the doors should have opened and the barriers between them should have come down. But somehow a new insecurity developed. Harrison and Amy feared the thought of ever losing each other, yet the divisive elements were still there despite all their efforts to accept and understand each other.

It was especially difficult for Amy because the more she explored the past, the more she found herself annoyed by the simplest things that Harrison was doing. Maddeningly she actually found herself yearning at times for the controlled and peaceful atmosphere of her fantasy about Harrison I. As she thought about the beautiful wedding she and young Harrison had attended together, she couldn't help imagining how it would really have been staged a century before. She also couldn't keep from picturing Harrison I as the bridegroom. He would certainly fit the part better than a man who wore electrodes on his head.

A few days later Amy was driving to the grocery store. She was engrossed in thoughts of Harrison, the warmth of his kiss still fresh on her lips. Strangely enough, his image began to remind her of the portraits of Harrison I, which she still studied and cherished. Suddenly a light next to the radio in her car came on, and a low voice addressed her. "You forgot your grocery list," it said sweetly. "Please stand by for transmission of same." To Amy's surprise a thin piece of paper resembling cash register tape filled rapidly with the items on her forgotten list, began to appear.

"No!" shouted Amy as though this were the final straw. Now not even the privacy of her car was safe. Harrison could intrude into her life anytime and anywhere he pleased with his crazy computers. She grabbed the list and flung it away derisively, and she knew the turmoil she felt was going to have to be addressed and addressed soon. When the little voice said, "Transmission complete, have a nice day," Amy slammed the dash of her car with her fist. "Go to hell," she shouted.

She had no idea whether Harrison could hear her or not, but she addressed him anyway. "We have to talk about this," she said, "as soon as possible . . ."

But before she could corner Harrison to talk to him seriously, fate intervened. When she arrived home, much calmer and admittedly grateful to have had the list of groceries, she unloaded the car and went to the mailbox. To her surprise, among the letters there was an old, obviously antique

160

postcard which was addressed to her house in the now familiar scratchy handwriting that she had seen on so many of Harrison I's papers. It was straightforward. It read:

Dear A.

Having a great time, but I miss you so much. Will be home soon,

Love, H.

She turned it over and felt a sense of déjà vu combined with an odd premonition as a warm rush went through her. The card had been mailed from Boston in 1906. How could it possibly be here now? She wondered. Her heart racing, Amy sank down on the front porch step and examined the card thoroughly. No doubt about it. There was the postmark, 1906, and there was no other. It was the most curious thing that had ever happened to her, and in spite of all her attempts to be rational, for a moment Amy honestly felt as if the postcard had been mailed directly to her.

She read the card again several times, and then the shock finally sent her racing into the house and up the stairs until she stood in front of the portrait of Harrison I.

"What is this?" she asked aloud as she examined the card and again recognized its authenticity and age. If this card *had* been mailed in 1906, why was it just arriving now?

Young Harrison found her in front of the portrait. "Amy?" he said hesitantly, deciding not to approach her. "What is it?"

She turned to him with a look of wonderment on her face. "I think Harrison the first has sent me a postcard," she said.

CHAPTER NINE

Young Harrison's breath caught in his throat when he saw the expression on her face. "What on earth are you talking about?" he demanded, walking rapidly across the room to grasp her by the shoulders.

"Here. See?" she said, holding the card up.

"Amy, for God's sake, will you listen to yourself?" He looked at her anxiously. "That's ridiculous, and you know it."

He gave her a little shake, and Amy seemingly came to her senses. "Yes, of course," she said, and began to daub nervously at the small beads of perspiration that had sprung out on her face. "It's just that this is the most curious thing."

Harrison took the card as a wave of rage and jealousy flowed through him. It was all that he could do to keep from ripping the card to shreds. "So it's an old card that was mailed by mistake," he said impatiently. "Surely there is a reasonable explanation."

"But it's postmarked 1906," she said, pointing to it. "There isn't any other postmark, and it's addressed to here."

"It should be very simple to check it out at the post office," he said as he handed it back. "You know for a moment there I thought I had lost you."

She flushed as she met his teasing smile and then looked away. "I know, I'm sorry," she said. "It's just that it was such a shock especially since it's addressed to A. I'd swear that it's Harrison the first's handwriting, and it just seems like too much of a coincidence."

"Well, what else could it be?" he asked. "I mean, let's be sensible. What if it is his handwriting? That makes sense if it's addressed to this house, and you did say his wife's name was Aribella, didn't you?"

The look on his face indicated that Harrison had gone about as far with this as he was going to go. "Well, this postmark *is* odd, though," she said as she examined the card again. "I'm going to check it out. This just might prove to be very valuable."

"Yeah, just think about the stir it would make at the open house," he said. "Harrison James the first sends greetings." He was relieved to see a normal reaction from her as he reached out to embrace her.

She loved the feel of his arms but still couldn't help a tentative look up at the portrait of Harrison I. Feeling her body grow tense, young Harrison looked up, too. "Ah, Amy," he said, smoothing her hair, "when is the competition between my ancestor and me going to end?"

She stepped back and gave him a questioning look. "What are you talking about?" she asked a bit nervously.

"You know what I'm talking about," he said. "And I think we should talk about it."

Amy couldn't believe how this frightened her. This was precisely what she knew needed to be done, yet something in her insisted that it was silly. After all, all she had ever had was a passing fantasy, something perfectly normal and healthy, something everyone had. "I think you're over-reacting," she said with a laugh. "The only competition between us is this crazy manipulating of yours which is making me uncomfortable in my own home." She paused and then decided to plunge on. "Like today—"

"What about today?" he asked slightly defensively.

"In the car," she said. "I felt my privacy had actually been invaded."

He looked at her questioningly.

She went on. "I mean, here I am, driving down the road, minding my own business, and all at once this voice intrudes—"

"Oh, you mean when I sent you the grocery list?" he asked, finally comprehending. "What was wrong with that?"

She already knew it was hopeless, but she was determined to try. "It's just that I'm not attuned to that sort of thing no matter how hard I try, and I just don't like it."

"I was only trying to help," he said, obviously aggrieved. "Weren't you glad to have the list?"

"Yes," she said in exasperation. "But that's not the point. Ever since the yard—"

"Aha!" he said as he began to walk around her. "I knew someday we'd get back to that."

Amy looked at him, a warning in her eyes, and Harrison felt his temper quickly die.

"I'm sorry," he said as he came back toward her. He reached out to grasp her shoulders. "I'm obviously being insensitive." He looked up and saw Harrison I again and seemed to delve a little deeper within himself. "I know I should remember that this is your house, I am, after all, only *renting* a room for the summer."

Amy couldn't believe the panic that began to beset her. "Now there's no need to get carried away," she said, and reached up to touch his troubled face. "I've never had such a wonderful summer, and I care for you very much. It's just that in some ways I'm still a very private person."

"And I'm intruding," said Harrison, giving the portrait one final belligerent look.

"No, you're not—I mean, yes, you are, but not in the way you think. Look, if you'd just leave the house and my car alone. I mean, don't do anything more than what you've already done. Why don't you just work on your serious experiments or the laser-X ray? You could try it out on the sundial. Maybe there *is* a time capsule."

"Oh, so now you admit that possibility," he said, suddenly victorious. A happy smile flitted across his face.

"Let's just say that I'm open to all possibilities." She tapped the postcard in her hand and gave him a calculating look. "There's something about this

166

card that's set me to wondering about a lot of things."

"All right," he said, and hugged her. "It's about time, and you've got a deal since all of my good Samaritan efforts seem to be bombing out anyway. No more tinkering in the house."

"Do you give me your solemn promise?" she asked, a wonderful wave of relief flowing through her.

"As solemn as I can get," he said, pulling her close. "You know, I think this is really going to be fun. I can't wait to examine the sundial."

"You will be careful now," said Amy. "I don't want anything damaged."

"Kid gloves all the way," he said with a smile as he looked at the four-poster bed and then at the portrait of Harrison I. "I think we ought to move that portrait," he added as they went out the door. "I'm getting a little sick and tired of always being watched."

"Now who's being silly?" said Amy as they descended the stairs. "You know, though, that reminds me of a story I saw once on television. It was about a woman caught up between lovers from the past and the present. In the end she chose to go back in time but sent a message to her modern-day lover through a portrait of her that was painted and hidden in a special place just for him. In it she wore a necklace he had given her, and that was her signal to him that she had been happy."

Harrison's steps visibly slowed as Amy told him this story. When they reached the bottom of the

167

steps, he turned her toward him and looked into her eyes. "You don't really believe in that kind of stuff, do you?" he asked, scanning her face with great seriousness.

"No, of course, not," said Amy, giving him an incredulous smile. "It was one of the most intensely romantic, touching stories that I have ever watched. Getting this postcard reminded me of it, and now I'm really wondering what might be in that sundial."

"Oh," said Harrison, his euphoria subsiding. Every time he thought he had really reached her, it was more evident than ever that he was sharing her with a ghost, a figment of her imagination. "Well, I hope you find what you're looking for," he said.

"Time enough for that," said Amy. "But first let's get the open house out of the way."

Moments later Amy was standing alone in the kitchen, reexamining the postcard. She knew it was silly. But what if there was something to all this?

For just a moment she could almost imagine Harrison I dropping that postcard in the mail when he had docked in Boston after a long voyage. Of course, he would have missed her, just as she had missed him. She could visualize herself getting ready for his arrival: the cleaning of the house, the cooking of his favorite foods, the choosing of just the right dress . . .

It was almost like old times, and suddenly Amy knew she could never stop loving the Harrison of her dreams. He was so wildly romantic, everything that she had ever wanted in a man. And it was so much safer and easier to live in a memory, in dreams of yesterday. The touch of him would be so wonderful; she knew it would. And there would never be all these crazy things to boggle her mind and drive her mad. For a moment she almost wished she could be that girl in the show. She almost wished she could really go back in time.

"Oh, my God," she said as she realized what she was thinking. She shoved the card into her pocket hastily and began to put away the groceries that she had brought in earlier.

Harrison was also a captive of his emotions, for he continued to feel a prickling of resentment. As he looked at all the antiquity that surrounded him, he began to wonder why he was trying so hard to prove himself a better man than his own great-great-grandfather. "This is utterly and absolutely ridiculous," he said out loud. "And I've got to put this into perspective for her once and for all."

With that he went up to the room Amy had given to him when he first arrived. It had long since become his laboratory and study, and he had to admit that he felt at home there, gazing out through the wonderful windows that surrounded it. Today, as he tried to think rationally about his problems with Amy, the marvelous vistas the windows offered of the sea were especially welcome. Finally, he picked up the laser-X ray and sighed. Somehow the prospect of using it to examine the sundial had lost a lot of its appeal.

For some reason their relationship was tarnished. He had a terrible feeling, almost a premonition, and suddenly he sighed in deep exasperation. He and Amy had been close, perfect, yet always far away. Today he was more sure of that than ever, and he longed for that moment at the wedding they had attended when everything had been so right.

The open house took place a few days later, and for a while it looked as if everything would go off without a hitch. Amy was beautifully dressed in a long, slender ankle-length dress that she had crocheted. It had tiers of fringe on the hem, wrists, and neck, and she looked like an authentic turn-of-the-century heroine. She seemed especially appealing with her hair parted in the middle and a little chignon at the very top of her head. Wispy strands of hair framed her eyes, which took on a slanted doey look above her high cheekbones and lovely patrician nose. Her demure little smile completed the effect, and Harrison had to admit that he had never seen her looking lovelier or more at home as she ushered people into the gleaming old house.

Everything was perfect from the proper little teacakes and the very correct punch she served down to the beautiful silver spoons she used. "Dear, this is just absolutely lovely," said Mrs. Donkenny, who politely paid her respects.

"I'll second that," said Lawrence, giving Amy a comradely squeeze. "Anything new?" he asked as he turned to Harrison.

"Just the same old stuff," replied Harrison with a bit of an aimless smile.

Amy smiled, too, but inwardly tensed. The uneasiness between her and Harrison had continued to grow. She had gone dutifully to the post office about the postcard only to be told in no uncertain terms that it had not been delivered by a modern postman. Just as she had noted, there was only one postmark and while the mail had often been the subject of late delivery stories, they told her a card could not possibly be held up for nearly eighty years. Amy couldn't say she blamed the people at the post office for their attitude, but at the same time she felt she had to find out how that card had landed in her mailbox. The only other explanation was that it was some kind of hoax, and that left her very uncomfortable. In the meantime, it was obvious that Harrison V was terribly sensitive about this, so they both had prudently chosen to ignore further discussion about it while they completed the details for the open house.

Amy was also confused by Harrison's sudden lack of interest in the time capsule after he had been so enthusiastic and insistent earlier.

With smile firmly in place, Amy was just giving mental thanks for the success of the open house when suddenly she heard a loud scream. To Amy's horror one of the long mechanical arms that Harrison had installed while she was away at the antiques show begun to unfold into the room. Before she knew what was happening, it was trying to grasp Mrs. Donkenny's dress. The frightened woman was screaming.

Harrison knew immediately what had happened while Amy's voice rang out to him in anger.

He raced to the kitchen. An astounded woman stood before the panel, which she had touched out of curiosity. Harrison had never completed this gadget, which had been initially programmed to activate only to his palm print, subject to entry of a specified female palm print. It was obvious that something was going wrong with it. Now, as some people ran round screaming, trying to get out of its way, while others laughed, the arm was waving around aimlessly.

"Harrison!" shouted Amy, who was sure she was going to die of mortification.

Quickly he deactivated the arm, but not before the tablecloth had been ripped from the table, sending food and punch all over the floor, and several of Amy's more valuable antiques had suffered some damage, not to mention the hysterics and outrage of several of her guests, Mrs. Donkenny among them.

"Oh, Harrison," said Amy as she began to cry, "how could you have allowed something like this to happen?"

"Now, now," said Lawrence, coming to comfort her. "There's no real harm done. Actually I'd say you've added a rather rousing element to this whole thing."

"Well, I wouldn't say that," said Mrs. Donkenny with a sniff. "You may be sure I will *never* come back to this house. I'm beginning to wonder if anything in it is what it is professed to be."

"Now just a minute," said Harrison as he came to Amy's defense.

"No, don't say anything," said Amy dully.

She took a big breath as the angry woman stalked out, and then Amy reached down deep within herself for a bright smile. "I'm so sorry," she said, trying to sound cheerful. "Harrison, you see, is one of the descendants of the original owner of this house, and he has . . . been . . ." She wrung her hands, trying to find some reasonable explanation, as her lips trembled. In that moment she was sure all her credibility was gone, and she was hurt and angry.

Harrison inwardly died, too, as she steadfastly avoided looking at him. He offered his apologies and went about solicitously comforting everyone while slowly the humor of the situation finally began to win out. While Lawrence went about cleaning up the punch and with Harrison's help righting the table, Amy managed to smile and thank everyone who offered her warm reassurance. She was happy to discover that many of them found Mrs. Donkenny more than a little bit of a stuffed shirt.

"Actually it's rather interesting," said a man to Harrison as he requested a look at the arm again.

In the end it was the understanding which was almost too much for Amy. She was filled with wrath and forced to smile and accept compliments when she really wanted to grab Harrison and pound him and his computerized mechanical arm right down through the floor. "Don't touch me," she snarled when he got a little too close to her on one occasion.

Harrison now felt terribly hurt, and although Lawrence continued to play the role of peacemaker, smoothing and guiding everything and everyone back into place, Harrison knew this was the end. The premonition he had been feeling ever since the arrival of that ridiculous postcard now seemed to be reality.

"I guess it's over," he said later when all the people had finally left.

To make the problem even worse, Harrison had slowly become a *cause célèbre*. As word of the incident spread among the people at the open house, everyone became fascinated by his experiments. Had it not been for Amy's wrath, he probably could have had a wonderful time explaining his inventions, but he had prudently tried to guide the interest back to the historical significance of the house and the event. Nevertheless, it was just one more thing that bothered Amy. She looked around the house and remembered all that it had come to mean to her and how hard she had worked to restore it, and she knew she had had enough. "Yes," she said, raising her head defiantly and meeting his gaze. "I've had enough of this."

Too late Harrison realized she was talking about them.

"What do you mean?" he asked, more agitated than he had ever been.

"I mean just what I said," she answered resignedly. "It's over. I want you to take all your little inventions and toys and get out of here—"

"Oh, you do, do you?" He was angry when he knew he should have been conciliatory. But he couldn't help himself. "Well, I'm through, too. You don't want a flesh-and-blood lover anyway. You'd

174

rather dream about a man who's been dead for nearly fifty years."

"You have your nerve," she said as all the anger she had held within her rushed out in a torrent. "You took over my house as if it were your own. And now, after you've made a shambles of my life and my house, you have the nerve to blame me. Well, let me tell you something. You're right. I do prefer my dreams about Harrison James the first. At least my dreams can't hurt me."

"Well, that's just fine. Keep on dreaming. Maybe someday you'll wake up and start living in the real world. Maybe you'll even realize that ghosts can't keep you warm at night. If that should ever happen, do me a favor. Don't give me a call!"

"Stop," she said as she pulled away from him. "You have no right to say such outrageous things." Tears were coming down her face.

"I don't want to say these things," he said, suddenly contrite, "but Amy, don't you see? My great-great-grandfather was a very married man, he loved his wife, Aribella, and I can't believe he would ever have wanted you to be a slave to an obsession about him."

"It's not an obsession," she said, glaring at him. "Can't you see, this is my interest? This is the way I want to lead my life. I can't stand having mechanical arms in my house that tear the clothes from my guests, and I don't like having my yard ruined by a runaway lawn mower. I want to live with and enjoy the simple old things. There's nothing wrong with that."

"Everything is wrong with that," he said derisively as he stubbornly stood firm. It was almost as if he felt he must overcome this obstacle once and for all, or all was lost forever. "There's nothing wrong with enjoying and studying history," he said, "but you refuse to live in today."

She glared at him, and he knew he had gone too far. "Oh, Amy," he said, reaching out to her, "all I want is for us to be happy together."

"Yes," she said as her eyes flashed. "Happy together, but only on your terms. You say I'm obsessed, but what do you think you are? You can't stand to leave anything alone. You think you can improve everything. I'm surprised you haven't added God to your name!"

They stood toe to toe as all the things they had been afraid to confront came tumbling out in wild, uncontrollable rage. Differences that might have easily been negotiated in a more reasonable atmosphere were now blown completely out of proportion. Harrison inwardly winced as her last words hit home, but his expression never changed.

"Well, I guess that's about it," he said, and his eyes grew hard. "It's been nice knowing you, *Miss Amy Kyles.*" His voice was dripping with sarcasm. "Maybe I'll send you a postcard sometime."

"You do that," she shouted as the door slammed behind him. "You just do that."

CHAPTER TEN

In the days that followed Harrison's angry exit Amy felt as if she were in shock, too numb to feel the full consequences of what had happened. She kept expecting him to come back and geared herself for an awkward confrontation that she knew would be almost too painful to endure. But he didn't come back. His clothes and belongings remained as he had left them, and the house grew eerily quiet as the projects that had once signaled his presence became reminders of the chaotic time they had spent together. But as the days lengthened into a week, Amy found herself growing angry again at Harrison's obviously high-handed and totally insensitive nature. His mean parting words echoed over and over in her mind, feeding a sense of outrage beyond any that she had ever experienced.

In view of her nature it seemed only natural that she would retreat to the fantasies she had once enjoyed. The postcard dwelt on her mind, and she again began to think about Harrison I and her strong feelings about the house. She went through all the papers and trunks that had been so fascinating, in the hopes that they would take her mind off her problems, but it didn't work. Just days after young Harrison's departure the doorbell rang and Amy opened the door to an obviously uncomfortable stranger.

"I do beg your pardon," he said. "I know this is going to sound terribly odd, but I was wondering if by any chance . . ."

He seemed to falter, and Amy gave him a questioning look. For a second she considered closing the door. But seeing her reaction, he quickly continued.

"What I'm trying to say," he said, "is that I'm a serious collector of memorabilia, and a few weeks ago I was mailing a large stack of brochures which were all packaged and sent by meter mail. I think my secretary may have inadvertently included an old postcard I had just received on consignment and was considering purchasing."

Amy looked at him and began to laugh as she thought of the ridiculous reaction she had had over the card.

"Fortunately I'd made a copy, and this was the address on the card," the man was saying.

"Come in," said Amy as she opened the door wide. "You know you managed to create quite a little stir around here."

The man had left awhile later, smiling and happy to have recovered a prize specimen after Amy had jokingly told him of her response when it arrived. She managed to make it so light and airy that she wondered now how she had ever allowed herself to have taken it seriously.

After that all her efforts to summon up old fantasies seemed somehow foolish. With the mystery of the card solved, the magic was definitely gone, and in that moment she knew the feelings she had shared with Harrison V were far more important to her than her dreams of life long ago. Although she still loved her surroundings, she no longer felt content. Even the big four-poster bed became cold and lonely. The long days began to feel like exercises in agony, but she stubbornly refused even to attempt to call Harrison although it was evident now that she would never have peace again unless they settled their differences in a satisfying way.

She suffered in quiet desperation as loneliness and a sense of loss unlike any she had ever known threatened to overwhelm her. She couldn't stop thinking of the first few days she had known Harrison V, remembering her shock over the uncanny resemblance between him and his great-great-grandfather. She touched the John Needles desk and recalled how casually Harrison had purchased it just so he could house his computer in it and appease her at the same time. Surely he wouldn't forget about that. He couldn't be that extravagant. Then she went on to the book about palmistry. Again she examined the broken lifeline in her palm and read about the "do or die" attributes that seemed to match Harrison's. She grew warm again as she remembered the tenderness of their nights together and the many other times when Harrison had declared himself to her. How could something so right and beautiful come to this? But

179

then she painfully remembered her growing dissatisfactions and the paranoia she had felt about his taking over what she had thought was her chosen way of life until she came at last to the dreadful confrontation after the open house.

In those terrible moments she was often tearful and racked with profound sorrow. At other times she got angry all over again. "Oh, damn him," she cried one time as she walked around the house and saw the craziness of his inventions. "Why did he ever have to come here? Why didn't he just leave me alone? I was perfectly happy."

But reason would prevail, and she would remember that *she* had placed the ad in the newspaper. *She* had prompted their first meeting.

At times she would have the strangest feeling that the relationship wasn't over yet, but somehow she wasn't looking forward to the final results either. She was almost afraid to think of how it was going to end. That's when she knew the real reason for her reluctance to find Harrison. So long as his belongings were there and no other arrangements had been made, he had to come back sometime.

Harrison too was suffering in a way that he had never expected. When he left Amy's house, he was consumed by his rage, and he simply drove around for the next two days, going without sleep and not eating, until he finally circled back to his apartment at MIT. There he couldn't concentrate on anything except his obsessive feelings about Amy and a sense of outrage that he had spent so much time competing with a long-dead ancestor.

At the same time he began to realize that his everyday way of thinking, which had always been admired and fostered in the strict cloistered atmosphere of his scientific world, could indeed have been a little overpowering for someone like Amy. He also realized, once he had begun to settle down and a shred of his earlier objective rationality had reappeared, that he loved her and wasn't going to give her up. He never gave a thought to going back to collect his belongings. On the contrary. With a sense of purpose unlike anything he had ever known, Harrison V set out to learn everything there was to know about Harrison I. More and more he felt a certain understanding of the man that went much further than just kinship. When he saw Amy again, he was going to be fully armed, and this time they were going to come to an adult understanding. This thing was going to be put to rest once and for all. Harrison thus set out to retrieve a complete family history, beginning with relatives and ending up in several prestigious libraries and museums, including the Smithsonian.

Amy in the meantime had begun to prepare for her fall classes at UMES. She tried to put her life together again and sought solace in her friendship with Lawrence.

"I've really blown it," she told him as they stood in her yard next to the sundial. She could feel tears in her eyes but managed to control them. "You know when Harrison talked about turning this into an atomic clock and looking toward the future, I didn't understand what he was talking about. Now I think he was probably right."

"Well, call him," said Lawrence. "Get it over with."

"I can't," she said. "I feel so foolish."

"Surely he's not going to leave all these things here," said Lawrence, who then puffed on his pipe. "Maybe I could get him to come examine this thing." He was looking at the old metal edges still protruding from the base of the sundial.

"Oh, no," she cried, chagrined at the very thought. "He'd see right through that."

"So what if he did?" said Lawrence. "Maybe he's waiting for something like that."

"I couldn't face him," she said hastily.

"All right, then let's examine the sundial ourselves. Something tells me this could be important to you."

"Well, it's already damaged," said Amy. "I guess there's nothing to lose."

So it was that several days later that a curious-looking pyramid-shaped container was removed from the sundial.

"Maybe we should wait for Harrison," Lawrence said.

"No," said Amy. "Let's take it someplace and have it opened. Even if we could X-ray it with Harrison's invention, we'd still open it, and I think this has gone on long enough."

Hours later she sat looking at the contents of the container, which indeed were part of an ingenious time capsule. Among the items was a letter from Harrison I. Tears ran down her face as she held it in her hand. She read the scratchy words which sent greetings to the future. He also wished fervently that his family would still be there in the house he loved.

Fleetingly she remembered young Harrison's words about preserving minds from the past in space age computer software, and Amy realized then for the first time that it was Harrison V who had embodied the true spirit of this man and his house. She looked blindly at a book of poems by Aribella and sniffed back tears as she also tried to comprehend the intricate drawings that were filled with lines and numbers.

"Oh, Lawrence," she said, dabbing at her eyes with a handkerchief, "I think I've made a terrible mistake from the very beginning."

After that she felt the presence of Harrison V's spirit all around her on a fairly constant basis. She tried to telephone him now, but to no avail. Once in a moment of real frivolity she had gone up to the round room and actually contemplated attempting to use the computer. Downstairs the John Needles desk seemed to mock her, and finally, on one occasion, she had turned the keyboard on and looked desperately into the screen. *Harrison, I need you,* she'd thought. *Please come back.*

But she didn't know how Harrison made the computer work with his mind. She didn't even know where he was.

While she made every effort to cope with her deep despair, Amy also lived with the continued sense of waiting for the other shoe to drop. Beneath all of this, almost like some inner ray of hope that somehow kept her from crumbling completely, she knew now she would give anything to have another chance. But her rational side knew this was far from probable, for the memory of Harrison's derision and anger never left her mind.

Then, the day before her classes at the university were to begin, there was a loud knock on the door.

"Amy Kyles!" a voice called out. There was a wild rattling and shaking of the door. "Amy Kyles, come and open this door immediately!"

For a second Amy was taken aback by his angry, strident voice, but she began to run as joy filled her body and lit up her face. "I'm coming," she called. "Just a moment." She took a quick glance in the mirror and was breathlessly fussing with her hair as she arrived. "Harrison . . ."

"Just open up," he said as he juggled an armful of papers and books.

She was taken aback by his appearance and manner but nevertheless rapidly opened the door.

"Now you're going to listen, and you're going to get this straight once and for all," he said. He marched past her, and Amy found herself trailing after him in total confusion.

"But there's no need," she sputtered.

"Oh, yes. Oh, yes," he said as he gave her a determined look. "I'm going to tell you all about Harrison James the first, and *you* are going to listen!"

"But—" Amy reached out to try to make him understand.

"Don't interrupt," he said sternly. "I insist that you give me a fair hearing."

Realizing it would do no good to protest, Amy sat back and reveled in the warm glow that began to travel through her. She smiled contentedly as Harrison began to spread the materials about.

"First of all," he said as he settled her into a chair and began to hand her his proofs, "Harrison was an inventor, considered somewhat of an eccentric in the family, but there are dozens of patents in the patent office bearing his name." He looked at her pointedly. "Do you know why those cast-iron pans you've been using were in the attic? Harrison invented lightweight ones for a cook who had arthritis! The Smithsonian has samples of some of his other ideas, and just as I surmised, he was indeed working on a primitive version of a computer. He was way ahead of his time, and this house is most definitely his handiwork."

"Harrison, I think I've already begun to realize—"

"No, wait. I'm not through," he said as he began to settle down a bit. "Where's that Bible?"

Amy handed it to him and couldn't hide the questions in her eyes.

"In addition," he said, scanning the pages, "Harrison James the first was a very good but stern father, and he worshiped great-great-grandmother Aribella. She was an artist, beautiful and exotic. She loved to wear kimonos and caftans and other creative types of dresses. She was probably bohemian before the term was ever known down here, and she painted the portraits of Harrison the first."

Yes, it all made sense now that Amy thought

about it. That explained the deep emotion that had always characterized the small portrait in the library. "But it seemed so obvious," she said, wrinkling her brow, "that Harrison was a sea captain—"

"That, my dear, sweet Amy, is the best part of all. He's wearing a *band* uniform in that picture. Harrison directed the local orchestra, and his hobby was writing music and directing lively marches in the town park during the summer."

He paused and looked at her very carefully.

Amy honestly didn't know what to say. The truth was that she was a bit dumbfounded as all her previous notions came tumbling down once and for all. Now, as the enormousness of all this began to overcome her, she looked away. "I guess this makes me look pretty foolish," she said. "And I suppose you'll be wanting to get your things together."

"No!" he said, his voice filled with emotion. "That's not what I'm saying. Amy, can't you see that I've spent all of this time getting this together because I love you? I can't live without you, but this misconception of yours was coming between us. Can't you see that I'm probably everything that Harrison the first was, but I want you to love me, just me?"

"I do love you," she said softly.

She opened her eyes wide and raised her head slowly until she was looking directly at him. "After you left, I knew I loved you and only you for who you are and what you are. I even tried to reach you through the computer."

"You did?" he shouted, his face filling with joy. "Oh, Amy, how could we have been so crazy about all this?"

"I don't know," she said, laughing as he pulled her into his arms and tumbled with her to the floor. "But I think it runs in the family."

He showered her face with kisses and caressed her with an easy familiarity. "So does this," he said as he pulled her to her feet and looked toward the stairs.

"No, wait," said Amy, who continued to laugh. "We have the rest of our lives to make love, but right now I want you to see what was in the sundial."

"You opened it? Was there a time capsule?"

"Oh, yes," she said, a note of seriousness in her voice. "There is a very touching letter from Harrison the first." She reached up to caress his face and willed him to understand. "We have to talk. We have to come to terms with our differences. I don't think I could ever bear to go through something like this again."

"All right," he said as he led her back to the couch. "But I can already tell you that in conducting this research, I've come to have a great respect for history. I can easily understand your interest in it now. Why, I've met relatives I didn't know I had, and I've even learned things that will help me with my work." A curious look came over his face. "In fact," he said as he suddenly arose, "I almost forgot."

Amy gave him a puzzled look as he raced out the door again. He returned with a strange-looking contraption in his hand. "Uh-oh," she said, recalling his earlier mad machines.

"No, it's not what you think," he said with a smile. "This is the loom that Harrison was studying for his computer theories, and I'll bet the full plans for it were in that time capsule!"

"You're kidding," said Amy.

"No," he said. "And guess what. This thing works. I know you'll love it."

"Oh," said Amy as she took a closer look. A definite hint of mischief crossed her face. "Looks like a lot of hard work to me. Are you sure you can't think of something to soup it up, maybe a light or something so all I'd have to do is look at it and think the pattern?"

The disappointment that had started to cross Harrison's face suddenly turned into a radiant smile, and the laughter in Amy's eyes matched that in his.

"Well, I think that might be arranged," he said, and reached out to pull her close again, "but only on the condition, of course, that I know exactly what's in your mind. I mean, I've got to get more than a little intimate with those brain waves to make something like that work."

His kisses were beginning to do his speaking for him as Amy gave into her own sensations. "Well, I think that might be arranged," she said with a low, throaty laugh, "on a strictly selective basis, of course."

"Good," he said as he scooped her into his arms. In swift movements he carried her up the stairs, strode into the bedroom, and then placed her gently on the bed. "Oh, Amy," he whispered as he looked down on her and she stretched with feline grace. "You're everything I've ever dreamed of. You've fulfilled every fantasy I've ever had."

"Aha!" she said. Her eyes narrowed, and her voice took on a sexy purr. "So I'm not the only one around here with an overblown imagination."

He smiled and melted into the very touch of her while his body lengthened next to hers. "Oh, no," he said, fingers beginning a questing trail. "Oh, no. I've dreamed of you and been driven by you. All these weeks I knew I should have called, but I was so afraid that it might really be over."

"Harrison?" She paused and held him at arm's length for a moment as her fingers dug into his hard, lean shoulders. "What are you really saying?"

"I'm saying," he said as he broke her hold and eased down onto her body with a sigh, "that I'm sorry I lashed out at you the way I did."

"You had every right," she said as she ran her hands through his hair.

"No," he said. "We could have talked it out."

"We weren't talking then," she murmured. His hands moved lower. "I know I hurt you, too. We both were being crazy, me with my fear of taking a chance and you—"

"With my paranoia and frustration." He finished for her. "Sometimes I felt so inadequate and you seemed so settled and happy, so sure of yourself yet so sweet and feminine . . . a dynamite combination." A sheepish little smile tipped the corners of his mouth. "At first, though, I figured I could easily win out over a ghost, especially if I came on as one of those pushy heroes in your books, and sooner or later I'd prove myself to you, but you know, when that postcard came, I began to have real doubts."

"You mean, you thought it was really from Harrison the first, too?"

"No, never," he said as he buried his face in her breasts. "I never for a moment thought it was anything like that."

"You did, too," said Amy with a whoop of triumph. "Harrison James, you are just as involved with the spirit of this house as I am, and you may as well admit it."

"I'll tell you what I'm involved with," he said with a growl as his eyes lowered and he pulled her beneath him. "I'm involved with making love to the woman I adore, who is also the woman of my dreams, and I have time for only one apparition at a time."

"Apparition?" echoed Amy, who began to work a little physical magic of her own. "Do you call this the touch of an apparition?"

Harrison gasped as her hands moved down over him, and then they both were lost in the throes of their passion as their bodies ignited into a fury of lovemaking. Reaching for every nuance of pleasure, Harrison searched every inch of her body, moaning as his lips suckled her breasts. His hands sank into moist recesses that left her gasping with pleasure. When they finally came together, their joy was nearly unsurmountable as they ravished each other in the ancient rhythm that brought with it the heady promise of a new life.

"Oh, I love you," moaned Amy.

"I love you too, Miss Amy Kyles," said Harrison as he twirled a lock of her hair around his finger. "Do you suppose there's room for one more extension to the Harrison James family tree in the Bible?"

"If not, we'll add a page," she said as she reveled in the warm feel of his loose embrace.

"On strictly authentic matching paper, of course," said Harrison with a chuckle. "You know," he went on, rising onto an elbow, "I do love this house and all that it stands for, all that you've done to it. And I'll do everything possible to help with the complete restoration of it, but there's one thing that has to go."

He paused as Amy followed his eyes to the portrait of Harrison I. They looked at each other meaningfully. Slowly Harrison arose from the bed and walked with purpose across the room. With very precise movements he carefully removed the portrait from the wall and set it outside the bedroom door.

"Now then, where were we?" he asked as he came back to her.

"Right here, where we both belong," she said with a mischievous pat on the bed and a twinkle in her eye. "Together again and alone at last."